Christine Pullein-Thompson has been involved with horses all her life—she opened a riding school with her sisters when she was fourteen. She started writing at fifteen and published her first book with her sisters Diana and Josephine. Christine has written more than 90 books which have been translated into nine languages. She is best known for her pony books but has also written the highly successful Jessie series about a dog and general fiction stories for younger readers.

Christine has four children and lives with her husband Julian Popescu in a moated Parsonage in Suffolk with two horses, a dog and a cat.

Other Pony Books by Christine Pullein-Thompson

Published by *Cavalier Paperbacks*

Stolen Ponies
I Rode A Winner
For Want of A Saddle
A Pony In Distress

THE LOST PONY

Christine Pullein-Thompson

**CAVALIER
PAPERBACKS**

© Christine Pullein-Thompson 1994

Published by Cavalier Paperbacks 1994
PO Box 1821, Warminster, Wilts BA12 0YD

Cover Design by Michelle Bellfield
Cover Photograph by Alistair Fyfe
Courtesy of The Infantry Saddle Club, Warminster

ISBN 1–899470–03–4

Typeset in New Century Schoolbook and Ottawa
by Ann Buchan (Typesetters), Shepperton
Printed and bound by
Cox and Wyman, Reading, Berkshire

CONTENTS

Chapter One

THE TRAIN JOURNEY

They looked round the room for the last time; it had been their home for as far back as either of them could remember—just the one room for the four of them, mother, father and the two children. Next door there was a tiny kitchenette and bathroom, nothing else.

"You've remembered to pack my little horse, haven't you, Mum?" asked Mick.

It wasn't much of a horse; it had come from Margate where they had gone once on an outing; but it was Mick's most treasured possession. His uncle Fred had been a stable lad, until he became too heavy; they had all been to his little bungalow one summer to stay. It was a visit Mick had never forgotten, nor had he forgotten sitting astride one of the racehorses, riding down the road one early morning with the sun behind him.

Katie was small, with short brown hair cut in a bob and blue eyes. She dreamed too of riding, though she hadn't a china horse like Mick. It was that dream which stopped her crying, now that the moment had come to leave. She could only think, perhaps we'll be able to ride there—at the house where they were to live temporarily with foster-parents, because now that they had twin baby sisters, the one room was too small for the family, and someone had to leave.

They had deposited the twins with a neighbour, and now the taxi was at the door.

"Yes; I've packed the little horse all right; and Katie's old doll," said their mother turning the key in the lock.

They went down the plain concrete stairs which served all the flats in the small block. Outside there was sunlight, which showed up the dust on the street and houses. A gust of wind blew a piece of newspaper under a cart pulled by an old grey with cow hocks, straight pasterns and swollen fetlocks.

"Mum, I must say goodbye to Nelly," shrieked Katie.

"You can't keep the taxi waiting."

But already she had flung her arms around the old grey pony. "Goodbye, Nelly goodbye. I'm sorry I haven't any carrots."

Mick joined her, in spite of his mother's entreaties. He had a small, determined face, with grey eyes and a firm chin.

"We'll come back some day," he said.

Katie was crying now silently into the grey's mane. It was no good pretending—the moment had come, she was leaving.

"Come on, will you. We'll miss the train. Really we will," called Mrs Smallbone, strange and a little uneasy in her best coat.

"Come on son," called the taxi-driver.

They climbed into the taxi, which was an old-fashioned one, with put-up backward seats.

"Now cheer up, Katie. It may not be for long. You know you like the country, and the Health Visitor says the Millets are very nice people; and think, you'll have a bedroom to yourself," said Mrs Smallbone, drying her daughter's eyes.

They were in time for the train. Mrs Smallbone paid the taxi-man while the children gazed at Molsworthy Station for the first time. They hadn't much luggage, just one dark blue case between the two of them, and a bag of food for the journey.

Katie had stopped crying by this time, and she clutched her wet handkerchief rolled into a tight little ball in her hand.

Mrs Smallbone found them a nearly empty carriage. "Now you'll be all right won't you? Look out for Mrs Millet. She's tall and kind-looking, with blue eyes, the Health Visitor says. Don't you budge from the platform until you see her, and don't go speaking to anyone—strange men especially." Mrs Smallbone kissed them. She was even resigned to losing her children to foster-parents like this. Only Katie could see the sudden rush of tears which came to her eyes as she prepared to go, and the small girl clasped the damp handkerchief in her hand with a firmer grip and with an effort stopped herself crying, Don't go, Mum.

"Well, all the best, Mum," said Mick, sounding more cheerful than he felt.

"We'll be over to see you as soon as the twins are just that much larger," said Mrs Smallbone. "Be good; and remember to do your best at school and write us a nice long letter once a week."

She stepped on to the platform and was gone.

"Cheer up Katie," said Mick. "Everything may not be so bad. There may be a racing stable along the street. We may be allowed a dog."

But Katie couldn't speak; all that mattered was that she was leaving her mother and home.

"And the Health Visitor says Mrs Millet's very nice, and the school's lovely," continued Mick, painting himself a rosy future, seeing horses coming home from morning exercise, someone giving him a dog, a puppy, saying "It's one of the best in the litter." He could see school too, himself sitting for the eleven plus, succeeding, going on to a grammar school. And then I'll be a vet, he decided, and saw himself in a white coat, bandaging a horse's leg, tending a sick dog, examining a cow. The train had started now; they were leaving home, beginning a new life, going to places they had never visited before.

"We're moving, Katie. We're moving," cried Mick. People were waving on the platform, but they couldn't see their mother. "I expect she's hurried back to the twins," Mick said.

Katie didn't answer; she sat in a corner seat, looking out of the window, seeing, not the disappearing platform but, the room which had been home to her as far back as she could remember. She saw the kettle boiling, tea on the table, thick slices of bread and butter, her father coming in, morning, getting up, school, the playground, her friend Sophie and there was no compensation for that.

"I wish the twins had never come," she said.

"Don't be silly," replied Mick. "Don't you see we

only have to find a nice house and a job for Dad and we can all be together again."

"I hadn't thought of that," said Katie, drying her eyes.

"Look. We're nearly in the country already; there are the gasworks, and look, can you see green, green grass?" They gazed out of the window, until Mick suggested looking in the bag, which they found contained sandwiches, little cakes, sausage rolls and two oranges.

They munched their lunch, oblivious of time, staring at the passing landscape. They had already stopped at three stations when Mick cried, "Piddington! We've arrived."

On each side of them were fields. Half a dozen horses grazed in one; a herd of cows in another. The air smelt fresh; leaves were turning gold in the autumn sunlight.

They stepped on to the small platform, watched the guard wave his green flag, the train going away. There was a woman in a smart suit reading a paper.

"She doesn't look like Mrs Millet, and her eyes are brown," Mick whispered to his sister.

Everything seemed very quiet to Katie; she was a little lost without any noise; at home the radio was generally on, or her mother was singing as she cooked, or lately one or other of the twins was usually crying.

Standing on the almost empty platform, Mick was suddenly afraid. Had he made a mistake? Surely they had said Piddington was the name? Then he saw a tall woman in a plain brown coat walking briskly along the country road towards the station.

"I expect that's her," he said to Katie. "Look over there."

What if she hates us? wondered Mick.

If only it was Mum thought Katie. They gave their tickets to the man by the gate. "Are you the two kids who are going to Mrs Millet?" he asked.

"That's right," answered Mick.

"Well, she's coming along now."

They stepped on to the country road. There were fresh hoof-marks on the verge, a bicycle leaned again a gate.

"For all we know she has horses herself," said Mick.

"I don't think that's likely," replied Katie.

Chapter Two

FOR THOSE WITH MONEY

"Hello. Let's see, you're Katie and Mick. I'm sure we're going to get on very well together." Mrs Millet took their case; she wasn't like their mother, more severe to look at, less resigned. "Did you enjoy your journey?"

They walked along the road together; the verge was still patterned by hoof-prints.

"Do people ride? Is there a school or something round here? A racing stable?" asked Mick.

"Do you ride then?"

"A little," replied Katie.

"I'm afraid you won't get much here. Riding is for those with money, and I don't suppose your mother will be sending you much, will she?" asked Mrs Millet.

Their faces fell a little. "Have you a TV and video?" asked Mick presently.

"Yes and we have a cat called Toby. I hope you will be very happy with us. The last child who boarded with us stayed right up till the time she was married—more than ten years."

It sounded a very long time to Katie—so long that she started to cry again.

"Well, we won't be staying that long. We only want

to find somewhere to live, then we'll be together again," said Mick.

"They all say that; but time flies and they're still here. You'll like it in time, you'll see. Well, here we are."

They had reached a tall semi-detached house. Mrs Millet opened the gate. There wasn't much of a garden—a few flower-beds in front, a vegetable patch behind, empty but for weeds and a few cabbages. "You'll be having the attics. That way you can make a bit of noise without bothering us too much."

It wasn't as they had imagined it would be. They had expected to see chickens in the garden, a dog welcoming them, the country smell there had been round their uncle's bungalow; instead, the house was fully carpeted and there was a front room which was never used.

Mrs Millet showed them the bathroom. "Baths every other night for you two," she said.

She left them in the attics. In both rooms there were religious pictures and plain black iron beds; but outside beyond the cabbages, there were fields which rose slowly to tall woods which waited to be discovered beneath a stormy sky.

"You don't think we'll stay here ten years, do you? I couldn't bear it. Really I couldn't," cried Katie, sitting down on one of the beds.

"Of course not," cried Mick briskly with a certainty he didn't feel. "We must think of here as our head-quarters—our base, if you like; from here we must begin our search for a house."

"I thought it would be all quite different. I thought we'd ride, and then I didn't mind so much. But there isn't a racing stable, and we haven't any money, and Mrs Millet obviously disapproves ..." Katie's voice died away on a note of despair.

"But we've only just arrived. After tea we'll explore, and who knows what we may find? Do you remember the hoof-marks along the verge? Well, we'll follow them."

"But what's the use? We haven't any money."

"I'm going to be a vet. I'm going to specialise in horses. Just to look at them, to watch them, is education for me," said Mick.

Looking round the room they were in, he wouldn't admit defeat. If he couldn't be a vet, he'd be a lad in a racing stable—he had decided that years ago.

"Which room do you want?"

"I'm not particular. You can choose," he said.

When they went downstairs tea was ready in the kitchen.

"Did you find everything you wanted?" asked Mrs Millet.

"Yes, thank you."

Mr Millet was there, sitting at the table. "Hello, kids," he said.

The afternoon had turned into evening. A row of washing hung now above the cabbages.

"We were wondering if we could go for a walk after tea. Would you mind?" asked Mick.

An enormously fat cat rubbed himself against Katie's legs. A radio played jazz music.

"To explore, you mean? Not tonight. You've had enough excitement for one day," replied Mrs Millet, pouring them each a cup of milk.

15

"You'll like to watch TV tonight, it's show jumping at Hickstead. My wife says you like horses."

"Yes, we do. We want to ride," answered Katie, her eyes lighting up.

"You need money for that. But you can watch it on TV for nothing, so cheer up, Katie," said Mr Millet.

They helped wash up until they heard hoofs clip clopping along the road; then they rushed to the window and saw a girl not much older than themselves riding one pony and leading another.

"She's got two," cried Katie, and they thought, it isn't fair. Why should she have two and us none? They still stood at the window long after the hoof beats had died away.

"If wishes were horses, beggars would ride," quoted Mrs Millet.

They were at a loose end. At home they would have been talking to their mother, fetching nappies for the twins, watching a stream of traffic pass the window.

"Do you think you'll like the country?" asked Mrs Millet.

"Yes," replied Mick. "I wish we could have some animals, though. Could we keep a dog here if someone gave us one?"

"Not with Toby; he wouldn't take to a dog."

"How would you feed it, anyway?" asked Mrs Millet.

"You mean we would need money?" asked Mick. He hated the word now . . . money, what couldn't he do with money?

They stood about getting in Mrs Millet's way, until her husband switched on the TV, and then suddenly

16

they were in the world to which they wished desperately to belong—there were the jumps, beautifully painted, the floodlit arena, the crowds and most important of all the horses. Each horse, as he entered the ring, seemed more beautiful than the last; Katie was certain suddenly that they would never ride; her hopes had died with the word, money. She could only think, this is not for us. We'll always be sitting at a TV, never on a horse. We'll never ride into a ring, nor along a road, nor across fields, nor anywhere else. She accepted it, in the same way as she had accepted that she'd never have dancing lessons as the little girl in the flat below theirs did, nor learn the piano.

But Mick entered the ring with each competitor, jumped the course and went out to a burst of applause. It was like a dream, a very happy dream, until Mrs Millet said, "Look there's David Smith." He returned to the room and reality, and knew that he had left home, that he was to live here with the Millets for countless days.

"I like him because he started from scratch. Everyone knows that. Listen to the crowd," said Mrs Millet.

David Smith looked young; he rode a bay with careless ease. "He runs the big stables at Littleheath. They say he's a first class teacher."

"Is Littleheath far away?" asked Mick.

"Twelve miles."

David left the ring to tremendous applause. "He's done it again. That's Tornado he's on," said Mr Millet.

He had jumped a clear round; and he had started

from scratch, Mick reminded himself. When the jump off came, Tornado entered the ring like an actress certain of admiration.

"She's a great mare," said Mrs Millet.

To Katie the evening was a little unreal. It seemed impossible that they had been at home with their mother in the morning, and that now they were sitting in this strange house watching TV. She felt lost and weary and frightened of the future, and Toby, sensing that she needed comfort, climbed on to her knee.

They watched David being awarded second prize; then Mrs Millet switched off the TV and made cocoa, and saw the children to bed.

Chapter Three

THE PONY

Katie couldn't sleep; she could see the outline of the window lit by the greyness of an autumn night. The house was asleep; she had heard Toby turned out into the garden, Mr Millet locking up, heard the bathroom taps running, doors being shut, the sound of people getting into bed, drowsy voices and then silence. She wished now that she had brought a book—or would Mrs Millet have seen the light shining across the cabbages in the garden? And then unmistakably she heard the sound of hoofs. She sat up. There was no sign of dawn yet; The hoofs were coming along the road. She slipped out of bed and went to the window. At first she couldn't see anything; then she made out the clothes-line and the tattered cabbages and the rickety fence beyond.

The hoofs had stopped; but a moment later she could hear the sound of something brushing through the weeds, and then without a doubt, a snort among the cabbages. She turned to find Mick already beside her.

"It's a pony. It's in the cabbages," he said.

"I know."

"What shall we do?"

They could see the outline of the pony now, his broad cheek, neat ears, fine legs and pulled tail.

"He's a beauty. Let's see if we can catch him," suggested Mick.

"We mustn't wake the Millets."

They found their clothes; a moment later they were struggling with the bolts on the back door.

"What are we going to do?" asked Katie.

"I don't know."

Mick was tingling with excitement. It was as though he had known all along that this moment would come, and it was their first night. Who could tell what other excitements the next few days might hold?

The bolt slid back; they went out in the garden, staring through the blackness of night at a pony which raised his head to look at them.

"Whoa, whoa little horse," said Mick, imitating his uncle.

"What are we going to do?" Katie was cold. We should have grabbed an apple on the way out, she thought. We haven't even a strap to put round the pony's neck. What are we doing here? She was lonely and a little afraid, standing there in a strange garden on her very first night away from home.

"Whoa, whoa little horse," said Mick again, and the pony whinnied, soft and low, in a tone of welcome.

He's not wild, at any rate, thought Mick. Perhaps someone's offering a reward for him. Perhaps he's a stray. After all, there are stray cats and dogs, so why not a horse?

And then behind them the lights in the house went on. "Look, Mick, look. Whatever will they say? She'll be angry," cried Katie.

"Don't shout so. They don't matter. It's the pony which matters. Can't you see that?"

There seemed no time to lose. Mick could see the pony clearly now; he was a chestnut, with a neat white star. He had seen the lights too, and now he was snorting, tense, ready to flee.

The Millets are going to spoil everything, thought Mick, advancing, saying, "Whoa. It's all right. Don't be afraid," talking in the voice he reserved for children much younger than himself.

There were voices now shouting into the dark.

"Get out of my garden. Leave him alone. Come back into the house. Where's a stick? Why aren't you in bed? You ought to be ashamed of yourselves."

Katie was running forward now, stumbling through the cabbages, feeling them bend and snap.

"It's all right. Don't be afraid," pleaded Mick.

The pony was staring towards the house with interest.

It's no good. Everything's awful. What will the Millets do? Will they make us stay in bed tomorrow? wondered Katie.

"Leave him alone," shouted Mr Millet, and then stones started to fly. The pony stood it for a moment, a puzzled look in his eyes.

"Don't, don't," screamed Mick. "You'll hurt him."

Katie had stopped in her tracks. She had been brought up to be kind to animals—"Never ill treat a dumb animal," her mother had said over and over again. They had put crumbs on their one window ledge for the birds in winter, taken buckets of water down the concrete stairs to Nelly on hot summer days, cared for a stray cat. But it wasn't only at home—at Sunday School the Vicar had told them about Francis of Assisi. Their uncle had loved the horses he cared for as a father loves a son.

"You're wicked," cried Katie. "Wicked!"

She felt like hurling the stones back at Mr Millet; and she knew suddenly of the gulf, there would always be between herself and Mick and their foster-parents.

The pony had turned now; the puzzlement in his eyes was replaced by fear. He galloped away across the garden, jumped the rickety fence and disappeared along the road.

"He's gone," said Mick. He was too bitter to say more. The arrival of the pony had seemed something of a miracle; now it was gone. He didn't want to look at Mr Millet, nor ever speak to him again. He felt limp with disappointment.

"Come in at once," called Mrs Millet.

The children turned back towards the fence. Katie was afraid; but Mick no longer cared what happened.

"Now listen, young lady. I won't have you speaking to me as you did just now. You speak respectfully as you would to your own father. Do you understand?"

"You cut his shoulder. I saw the blood as he galloped away. We could report you to the RSPCA," said Mick.

He had to stick up for his sister—it was automatic, he always had. And, anyway, what he had said was true—he had seen blood on the pony's shoulder, a vivid red streak.

22

"He may die of tetanus, and it'll be your fault," he said.

"Fancy stoning a dumb animal," exclaimed Katie.

"People should look after their animals. Look at the damage that horse has done to the garden. Now come in at once and go to bed, and don't let me ever hear you address Mr Millet like that again," said Mrs Millet.

"If it wasn't your first night here . . ." added her husband.

They went indoors. The kitchen was too tidy and polished to be friendly.

"If we cared to report you, we could have you removed to a home, put in the care of the Council," said Mrs Millet.

There was no comfort anywhere. Katie hated the house. At that moment anything seemed preferable to life with the Millets.

The sound of hoofs had died away; only Mrs Millet's voice went on. "So you had better mend your ways," she finished.

The children went upstairs to the attics.

"I hate them, Mick. Really I do," exclaimed Katie. She couldn't restrain her tears; they streamed down her face in a seemingly endless torrent. She would have given anything to be back in the familiar room she had called home for so long.

"Don't cry. It won't help, and she'll hear." Already Mrs Millet had become 'She' to the two children.

"How could he stone the pony," asked Katie through her tears.

"They're regular church-goers too," said Mick.

But now they could hear footsteps on the stairs.

They were both apparently asleep when Mrs Millet surveyed the attics. She sighed with relief.

"We're going to have trouble with those two," her husband had said.

"I can manage them. We've had difficult ones before." She had said it with a certainty she didn't feel. She wasn't happy herself about Katie and Mick. They had an air of determination about them, they were individuals, not like the usual run of children from over-crowded homes.

Now she switched off the passage light and went downstairs.

"They're both asleep," she told her husband.

I'll shoot that pony if he gets into the garden again," said Mr Millet.

On the top floor Mick tapped three times on the wall.

"Cheer up, Katie. It'll seem better in the morning, really it will," he said.

But she was already asleep, the bedclothes pulled over her face, shutting out the unfamiliar room.

Mick tossed and turned, seeing the pony again, his dark mane and tail, his well-bred head lit by the solitary white star on his brow.

He wasn't despondent; he wasn't like that; for him there was always hope, a new start waiting round the corner; he wakened each morning to a new day with a sense of adventure.

And when he fell asleep at last as dawn crept across the lightening sky there was a smile on his face.

Chapter Four

THE SEARCH

Katie awakened to a knock on her door.

"Breakfast will be ready in five minutes," said Mrs Millet.

She jumped out of bed, gazed at the garden and saw that the hoof-prints were still there, vivid and deep in the damp earth.

"Remember to clean your teeth," called Mrs Millet. "There's a tube of toothpaste in the bathroom."

She heard her feet clattering down the stairs. Outside it was a typical autumn day: a heavy mist hung over everything; the trees were decorated by cobwebs and glistening wet leaves.

Looking out of the window, trying not to think of home, Katie thought about the chestnut pony which had visited them in the night. Where was he now? Where had he come from? Would they ever see him again? This morning everything which had happened in the night had the substance of a dream, but the hoof-prints among the cabbages told a different story.

I don't believe we'll ever ride, decided Katie, and then Mick came into the room already dressed, with a look of adventure in his eye.

"Hurry. Quick. Dress. Can't you smell the bacon and eggs cooking downstairs? We'll be late."

He knew it was Saturday; the whole day lay in front of them; anything might happen.

"We can follow the hoof-prints. The pony must have gone somewhere," he told Katie. "I'm going down. Don't be late or she'll be cross."

"Remember to clean your teeth," Katie called after him.

She found the dungarees she had worn when they stayed with Uncle Fred. They were rather short now, but she put them on just the same, and found a shirt, jersey and pair of shoes.

The house still smelt unfriendly as she went downstairs, in spite of the bacon and eggs cooking in the kitchen.

No-one mentioned the adventures of the night. The children ate stolidly. It was a good breakfast, better than they had at home, except for Sunday, when their mother always cooked something special.

"Can we go out this morning?" asked Mick.

"Yes, but be back for one o'clock lunch," replied Mrs Millet. She plied them with food, while outside the mist cleared, to be replaced by sunshine.

"Where are you going? Don't get into any mischief," said Mr Millet. He couldn't trust them now, not after last night.

"And tomorrow you go to Sunday School. The Vicar's expecting you," said Mrs Millet.

At last they were outside in the sunshine, with the smell of the country all about them.

"Let's find the village first," suggested Mick.

"If there is one . . ."

"Of course there is. If there's a Sunday School,

26

there's a church. That stands to reason . . ."

"What about the hoof-prints?"

"Leave them till after."

They walked away from the direction of the station along a twisty road with hedges on each side, and deep, dark ditches. It was all very strange after the large dirty industrial town where they had lived. The leaves on the trees were russet and gold, and already in places they carpeted the road, a lovely orange fringe on the tarmac.

"I feel so happy, except when I realise that we're far from home. Why can't one have everything?" asked Katie smelling the air.

"Perhaps we will one day."

People looked at them curiously when they reached the village. They found the church, the school alongside it and then the blacksmith's forge, the unmistakable smell of burning hoof, which they remembered from the racing stable, the ring of hammer against anvil, the sound of a horse stamping on a wood floor.

"Perhaps the blacksmith knows about the pony. He must know all about the ponies round here," said Mick, who once had wanted to be a blacksmith himself, before the urge to become a vet had ousted all thought of other careers.

A girl held a piebald pony, while the blacksmith rasped his hoofs. They stood in the doorway watching, waiting for an opportunity to speak.

The blacksmith smiled. "You'll be the kids lodging with the Millets . . ."

Mick nodded. "That's right," he said.

27

The girl wore a riding jacket, skull-cap, shirt and tie, well-cut jodhpurs and boots. Katie devoured the clothes with her eyes.

"I don't envy you," said the girl.

"A pony was in the garden there last night. Churned up Mr Millet's cabbages proper. Do you know to whom he belonged?" asked Mick. He wanted to ride himself unbearably now. Looking at the piebald brought a lump to his throat. His legs ached for the feel of a saddle. "A nice little chestnut," he added.

"Mr Millet must have been angry. You should have seen him one day when the Hunt went through. I jumped right over his fence and one of the hounds turned out his dustbin. He chased us out with the broom, and threatened everyone with the police," said the girl.

"Well, you shouldn't have gone through. Strictly speaking, it wasn't necessary, was it now?" asked the blacksmith, straightening his back. "Now what about the pony, son? A chestnut you say."

"With a star," added Katie.

"A good looker," said Mick.

They both felt at home here, and they remembered that their father had come from a cottage in the country. What had taken him to a town? wondered Mick, feeling that nothing would make him leave the country once he was old enough for a job and a home of his own.

"What sort of size was he? He wasn't a horse, was he?" asked the blacksmith.

"No, a pony, quite a little one," replied Mick, finding a blade of grass to chew.

28

The blacksmith couldn't help them.

I don't know a pony like that round here, not a chestnut with a star. Perhaps you ought to tell the police, though he might be a gipsy pony; we get the gipsies camping on the heath sometimes at this time of year."

"It didn't look like a gipsy pony," said Katie.

The children watched the pony shod, the girl mount and ride away; then they went back through the village, ignoring the children who gazed at them curiously as they passed the village shop.

They ate a substantial lunch.

They both felt they had a purpose in life now. They helped to clear the table; then they were outside again in the soft sunlight following the hoof-prints out of the garden away across a field of stubble.

"What are we going to do—if we find him?" asked Katie.

"I don't know . . ."

The feeling of prickly stubble was new to them; so was the horizon, the rising fields topped by woods, the space, the smells . . . Home was forgotten as they ran across the stubble in search of the chestnut pony; only adventure lay ahead.

"We may find where he lives," said Mick, "and then I shall say: I want to be a vet. May I study your pony? I want to be an expert on horses, and one day I shall write a great book called, 'The Horse from Beginning to End.' And they'll say . . ."

"It might be a riding school where we'll be able to help," interrupted Katie.

"And get rides in return." added Mick hopefully.

They were filled with great optimism, until they reached a road and saw that the hoof-marks had vanished, that there was no clue to tell them where the chestnut pony had gone. Katie could have cried then, but Mick said: "I've got an idea. Why not pretend that he's our pony?"

"Our pony?"

"Yes, stop people and say, Have you by any chance seen a chestnut pony?"

"Wouldn't that be wrong?"

"Why should it?"

"Supposing we asked the people he belonged to? . . ."

"Either way they should be pleased. After all, it must be quite a help to have other people looking for your lost pony," replied Mick stoutly.

"I'm sure Mum wouldn't approve."

"She isn't here. Anyway, it's not telling lies. After all, the pony came to us in the first place."

"As though he knew we wanted him."

"If you like to put it that way."

"It's wonderful, isn't it? How did he know? And horrible Mr Millet drove him away," said Katie, who believed in miracles.

"Let's hurry," cried Mick. "Look, there's a postman emptying a letter-box. We can ask him."

They started to run along the road, Katie's knees fighting the tightness of her jeans, Mick's thoughts racing ahead into the future, seeing the chestnut pony, no-one claiming him, the police saying, "He's yours. We've kept him a month and no-one's come for him." He didn't know the law about stray animals, except that dogs were destroyed after a certain time, or sent to the Battersea Dogs' Home, where they found new owners and new lives. He saw himself riding the pony, a meet of hounds, a beginning of another life for himself and Katie.

The postman was approaching now in his red van. Mick held out his hand.

"Have you seen a chestnut pony, please?" he called.

We shouldn't be doing this, thought Katie. It's wrong. I know it is. What would Mum say? But now the van stopped.

"What did you say?" called the postman, who was young and jaunty, smiling, with his cap on one side.

"Have you seen a chestnut pony around these parts?" asked Mick.

"A pony ... loose, you mean, of course .... No. Have you lost one?"

He seemed to be looking at them curiously. We aren't dressed in the right way, thought Katie, remembering the girl in the forge, and her heart started to beat furiously against her ribs, and she thought, we're playing with fire as Mum would say.

But Mick saw nothing wrong. "That's right. We're looking for a chestnut gelding with a flaxen mane and tail." He was proud of his knowledge. At least he hadn't said long hair, as many of the boys at his school would have done.

"I should try the post office further down; they're shut, but if you knock at the side door, someone will come. They don't miss much," said the young postman, starting his engine again.

They watched him drive away. "It's getting late," said Katie.

31

They started to run. The road was narrow, little more than a lane in places. They didn't stop at the post office.

"We don't want everyone staring at us . . . calling attention to ourselves won't do us any good . . ." exclaimed Mick as they ran past the shuttered windows, the lettering which said Rushcombe Post Office.

He felt that they had to hurry. They had spent a long time crossing the stubble; lunch had been late, and evening was coming early to the October day.

He couldn't bear the thought of returning to the Millets without success to comfort him.

"We're sure to see him soon," he shouted over his shoulder to Katie, who was dropping behind.

And then unbelievably they saw hoof-prints leading down a lane, which was fenced on each side by high hedges thick with brambles.

"There. What did I say?" said Mick beginning to run.

"But it may be a different pony. It's getting so late. Shouldn't we go back?" Katie saw Mrs Millet, her face red with anger. She'll send us away, she thought, and poor Mum will be so upset. "Mick, it's late," she called again.

But Mick saw only the chestnut pony, unwanted, lost, unclaimed. He saw them riding every afternoon, and beyond that he saw nothing.

"Come on. Run, can't you?" he shouted back.

Chapter Five

THE FIND

The lane grew wilder, more remote, until there were woods on each side, carpeted with moss, and now the children were running on flint and chalk instead of gravel.

"Look. There's a house," shouted Mick.

They had seen no sign of a pony for some time, but hoofs could cross the chalk and flint, leaving no mark behind. Katie's anxiety was rising with the gathering dusk.

"I can't see it. Where?" she cried.

"There, you twit." Mick stopped to point.

It was an elegant timber bungalow, with enormous windows, a conservatory and a tennis court.

There was a stable and behind it a garage. So cars do get up here, thought Mick. It looks like a film star's place—belongs to somebody with money at any rate.

"So what? There's no pony as far as I can see, and the house looks empty." Katie sat down. She felt very disagreeable. "We'd better go back," she said.

But Mick still stood looking at the house and now he could see something moving in the garden.

"There's something there. I'm not going back till I've looked. You needn't come if you don't want to."

"I'm not going back to face the music by myself. I said ages ago that we ought to go back, and it's nearly dark."

They stood quarrelling for a moment, until the moving thing in the garden turned its head and they saw quite clearly the outline of a pony. They began to run then, and gradually the pony took shape and they saw that he was chestnut and small, the visitor of the night before.

The gate into the garden was hooked back, the house obviously empty, since no smoke came out of the chimney stack. Mick and Katie broke into a walk.

"Whatever is he doing here?" asked Mick.

They could only guess. "Perhaps he lived here once," suggested Katie.

"Or strayed here and liked the look of it."

"There's not much grass."

"But there's a stable by the garage."

They started to run again, and the pony, seeing the children, whinnied and cantered towards them.

It's like a miracle, as though God knows how much we've always wanted a pony, thought Katie, and sent us this one.

I knew we'd find him if we looked long enough, thought Mick.

The pony stopped beside them, nuzzled their pockets.

"He's glad to see us. He knows we're his friends."

"Do you think he has a name?" asked Katie.

"I suppose so. I wish we had brought him something."

"He looks as though he was well cared for before he strayed. Let's investigate the stable," suggested Mick.

It was a solitary wooden loose-box. The pony pushed at the door with his nose. The children opened it. He walked in and hurried to the manager. He looked inside, then he whinnied to the children.

"There must be food somewhere. Come on, let's feed him. It'll soon be dark. Come on, Mick." Katie was exasperated with her brother, who would only stand and stare at the pony as though nothing else existed—certainly not an irate Mrs Millet, who with one well-written letter, or one brief telephone call, could send them away, perhaps to a home, perhaps to other foster-parents.

"He's so good looking, like the pony which won at Wembley last year. I must bring my book over tomorrow. Then we can find out his age by his teeth."

Mick's book was tattered and red, entitled The Everyday Farrier. He had found it on a bookstall standing in the market on a clear summer day. It was at least ninety years old. In it, farriers attended the sick horses in top hat and black coats. There were many lurid pictures, but to Mick it had opened a new world. Often his mother would say, "For goodness sake throw away that tattered old book. Why you want to read it I don't know." But he clung to it, kept it with his other precious possessions.

There was a lean-to shed next to the loose-box, where they found three bales of hay and a bin half-filled with oats. They found a bucket in the garage standing under a tap.

"Everything's here. It is like a miracle," said Katie.

35

They gave the pony half a bale of hay, a bucket of water, a manger of oats. They shut the loose-box door.

"He should be all right now until tomorrow," said Mick. They stood and looked at the pony for a moment while he munched his oats.

"I wish he was ours," sighed Katie.

"Perhaps he will be one day if no-one claims him."

"Someone's sure to. we'd better hurry back."

Katie was frightened again now. "We'd better start," she cried, running away down the drive.

It was dark, and here there were no street lamps to light their path.

"We must hurry. It's late, I know it is."

"So what? I'm not frightened of Mrs Millet," Mick boasted.

The lane was very dark, brambles clutched at their arms and hair. "We must try and get over early tomorrow," said Mick. "I want to try riding. Did you see the saddle and bridle at the back of the shed?"

"But he's not ours."

"Well, we're looking after him for someone. He's better there than roaming the roads, being run over, causing accidents!"

"Or being stoned by Mr Millet," Katie added.

And if he's capable of that, he's capable of anything. What will he do when we get back? wondered Katie.

They reached the road.

"Anyway we can't afford to miss such a chance. We'll groom the pony and look after him, so that he looks like a prince."

"Let's call him that—Prince. It's a lovely name," cried Katie.

So they called the pony Prince, and hurrying along the road chattering, they missed the stubble field and after a time reached a village which neither of them had ever set eyes on before.

"Oh, whatever shall we do?" cried Katie.

"Ask the way," replied Mick firmly. He knew his sister was near to tears. It was very dark, and they were not accustomed to it. At their parents' home a street light stood outside their windows and for hours it shed a warm glow through the chinks between the curtains, and when the small hours came and the street lamps went out, there was still Mum and Dad in the room, and more recently the restless twins as well, waking up to be fed at two. In the morning Mick wasn't afraid; only tense and alert.

"It's my fault, and I'm going to admit it," he said.

"It's mine too."

"I'm not afraid of the Millets. I'm the eldest too," said Mick.

"It doesn't make any difference," replied Katie.

They braved a dark garden and knocked on the front door of a large, many windowed house. A crescendo of barking greeted them. An elderly woman opened the door, holding back two Boxers, peering at them through bifocals.

"We're lost. Can you tell us the way to a village near Piddington, please?" asked Mick bluntly.

"Near Piddington? Oh dear, you'd better come in. Peter, Peter. These children come from Piddington."

"That must be Heelstead. All right dear. I'll get the car out."

"Come on. Don't stand out there in the cold."

She beckoned to the children into a cold, high, bleak, old-fashioned hall.

"Come into the sitting-room while my husband gets the car."

"But we don't expect to be taken home; really we don't." They stood blinking in the sudden glare of the lights.

"But you can't walk back there tonight, my dear children," said the elderly lady, releasing the Boxers, who fell to licking the children's hands.

They heard a car horn. "There he is. Now run out and jump in, there's good children. My husband will run you home."

"Can you manage? Lift the handle up," said the man inside as Mick struggled with the door handle.

They both forgot their mother's constant and often repeated warning, "Never take a lift from strangers."

They sat in the back and saw that their driver was very tall and that he wore a clerical collar.

"Are you new to these parts? I don't seem to have seen your faces before," he said.

"We're lodging with Mrs Millet. We came yesterday," explained Mick.

"You certainly are new, then. Do you like it?"

"Not much. We're really looking for a house. You see, if we can find a house we can all be together again. We found one this afternoon—an empty one, I mean. Do you know it, sir? It's at the end of a lane."

"Oh, you mean Four Ways. But it's a luxury residence—awful place, ruins the landscape."

Mick was rather taken aback. He liked the bungalow. "It's got a loose-box, anyway," he said.

"Yes; that's something. The place belongs to a couple of film stars. They've got a little daughter, a nice kid. The loose-box was for her."

"You mean she had a pony," cried Mick. Both the children were excited now.

"Yes, a little chestnut. She used to ride him through the village. I don't know what they did with him when they left."

"Where did they go then?"

"Hollywood, I suppose. Well, here we are. Which house is it?"

The journey had ended much too soon for the children.

"Tell us some more about the film stars," pleaded Katie.

"You're late enough, already. Would you like me to have a word with Mrs Millet, do a little explaining?"

They all went up to the house together. The children could see now that their companion was old and rather bent. They didn't speak; quite suddenly they were filled with dread. The path to the front door seemed unbearably long; only the tall figure of their new-found friend striding ahead stopped them faltering. We haven't planned what to say, thought Mick, and whatever happens we can't mention the pony—not after last night. Katie wanted to run away; anywhere at that moment was better than the tall, semi-detached house and a furious Mrs Millet.

They saw the lights go on in the hall as their friend

pushed the doorbell. Mick stood remembering the pony; at that moment he felt ready to die for his ambitions; whatever happened, he had to get through his exams and reach the Royal Veterinary College; and somehow, somewhere, he felt the pony would play his part. Katie saw them being sent home, her mother's worried face; the Health Visitor calling, saying, "Well, really, I don't know what to do next, Mrs Smallbone." Her father coming in; the twins crying, the kettle boiling over . . . her mother saying, "Why did you have to do it? Now see the mess we're in . . ."

Mrs Millet had opened the door, sending a shaft of light across the small garden.

"Why, it's Father Ambrose. Come inside," cried Mrs Millet.

"Come on, children" said their new-found friend. "These poor kids were lost, so I brought them home," he told Mrs Millet. "I should think they need a good tea."

There was no unpleasantness and the children's anxiety ebbed away. There was no mention of the pony.

Father Ambrose patted their heads and departed.

"Fancy you meeting him," said Mrs Millet. "He preaches here sometimes when the vicar's away."

Their places were still laid at the kitchen table. They ate a good tea. "And now half an hour's TV before baths," said Mrs Millet, washing the tea things.

After their baths they had a short discussion in Katie's room.

"We must try to slip away directly after breakfast,"

Mick said parting the curtains to stare into the dark garden outside.

"I hope we can find the way there," replied Katie, who was already in bed.

"We'll do that all right, and then we'll ride. Think of that, ride. Isn't that marvellous? We'll take it in turns. Do you remember how you trot? You know, up and down—like Uncle Fred taught us."

"Yes. But I hope it's all right. I mean, he isn't our pony."

"Oh stop worrying."

"Shouldn't we tell the police?"

"Well perhaps later, but first let's ride," said Mick, seeing them trotting up and down the drive at Four Ways, feeling the little chestnut pony's stride, the saddle flaps between his knees, the stirrups beneath the balls of his feet.

"Oh we're lucky, Katie," he cried. "Fancy finding a stray pony our first day in the country."

"He must have sensed we wanted him. That's why he came here last night." Katie was very sleepy. Now that she was in bed, the day behind her seemed one of the longest of her life.

"Supposing Mrs Millet won't let us go out tomorrow?" she asked.

Mick didn't answer, because already his mind was far away: the pony had become theirs, he had written to his mother saying, "We have been given a chestnut pony and we have called him Prince." He could see her opening the letter, the surprise on her face. Everyone would be pleased, the neighbours, his parents, even the twins when they were older and could understand. "Well, good night, Katie," he said, creeping on tiptoe from the room, because Mrs Millet had said, "No chattering, no banging on walls. You're in bed to sleep," before she had shut their doors, and clattered down the attic stairs to join her husband in front of the TV.

Mick found his bed, climbed inside. He thought, tomorrow we're going to ride. I'll ride first because I'm older and the pony may buck, and I'm bigger and stronger than Katie. I hope Prince is all right. We didn't leave much water for him. I wish I knew more. I must remember to take my book; and then he fell asleep.

Chapter Six

I CAN RIDE

"Wake up. Wake up, can't you," said Mick.

Katie opened her eyes and remembered—they had found the pony, called him Prince, been brought home by Father Ambrose; and this was another day, Sunday. "I'm awake," she said sitting up. "But it's still dark."

"That's the idea," answered Mick. "She didn't say we couldn't go out today, so let's go now before she has time to object. It's getting light. Look," he cried, drawing back the curtains. "And they're sure to get up late, because it's Sunday. We can go now, ride, feed the pony and still get back for breakfast."

So five minutes later they were outside in the clammy October dawn. Around them trees dripped, the grass was wet against their knees; the brussels sprouts drooped; washing hung sodden on the line.

"It's a good thing we put him in. It must have rained a lot in the night," said Mick.

They started to run across the stubble, guided by a faint light in the East. Katie's jeans were wet by this time, and her feet were soaking inside the white trainers she had put on. But she didn't care, because this morning she was to ride, and that was a dream come true. And if we never ride him again, we will still have had our pony and ridden him how we liked just once, she thought, and as she ran she smiled. "Oh Mick isn't this lovely?" she called.

"What?"

"Everything."

Mick's mind was already ahead, seeing other days, making plans, facing opposition, triumphing.

"We'll have to ride in the dark tomorrow, after school," he said.

"I wonder what time school comes out."

Dawn had just come when they reached the road beyond the stubble. They were both out of breath.

"Let's walk," suggested Katie. But they couldn't walk for long; suddenly there seemed so little time, so much might happen during the next few hours: Mrs Millet might lock them in their rooms when they returned, the film stars might be back in England, they might turn up and find them riding Prince; by nightfall anything could have happened. So they ran, splashing through puddles in their thin shoes, turning down the lane with a flourish, seeing Four Ways and, best of all, a neat chestnut head looking over a loose-box door.

"He's still there!" cried Mick.

They felt then, for a moment, almost as though he was really theirs, as though he would be there waiting for them every day for as long as they wanted him.

They stood and looked, and saw that the luxurious bungalow was still empty, that nothing stirred in the garden, that all was still as it had been the evening before.

"Come on," cried Mick.

They ran on up the drive past the neglected flower beds, the unmown lawn. The pony whinnied to them.

"Oh, Mick, he remembers," cried Katie.

She kissed Prince under his well-pulled mane, while Mick fetched a small feed of oats and a dandy brush.

"Will you groom or muck out?" asked Mick.

"I don't mind."

"You'd better groom, then."

They worked furiously, against time, against Mrs Millet getting up, finding them gone. They felt that they had their share of good fortune already, that there couldn't be much left for them.

Mick threw the dirty straw outside the door, collected the hay Prince had trodden round his box and piled it in one corner, washed out the water bucket and refilled it. Katie groomed Prince with the incompetence of the inexperienced.

She used her pocket comb for his mane and tail until all the teeth in it were broken.

"Come on. That's enough," cried Mick as he put down the water bucket. "We'd better try to put his saddle and bridle on."

The tack was very stiff. "It can't have been used for a long time," said Mick.

"I hope we can get it on."

"Of course we can."

The bridle was a snaffle. "First we put the reins over his head, then the bit in his mouth," announced Mick, taking one snaffle ring in each hand.

Prince stood patiently with a long-suffering look

on his face. Mick put the snaffle in his mouth, but every time he tried to pull the headpiece over Prince's ears something went wrong and the bit fell out of the pony's mouth.

"Can't you hold it in, Katie?" cried Mick.

They became hot and flustered and after a time Prince became impatient; he put his ears back, snapped and then began to stick his nose in the air so that they couldn't reach it.

"We'll never ride," cried Mick. "Will you stand still, Prince?"

"It's no good getting cross. He was so good at first. It's our fault," said Katie, who felt like crying with exasperation. And all the time minutes were passing; it was almost as though a clock ticked in the background, slowly announcing each lost second. "We'll never have time to ride," cried Mick, losing his temper suddenly and flinging the bridle across the loose-box.

"Oh, don't," cried Katie. "You're frightening him."

"Mrs Millet is probably up by now," said Mick. "At this rate we won't ride at all." He kicked the straw. He had planned it all. They were to have ridden up and down the drive, first at the walk, then at the trot. Each time they would have improved a little; now everything was ruined.

"Can't we ride him in a halter?" said Katie.

She put the saddle on, pulled up the girths.

"I'm sure it's too far back," said Mick.

She ignored her brother, found a halter, and a handful of oats. "Whoa, Prince, whoa," she said. She slipped the halter on quite easily, gave Prince the oats. "I'll go and shut the gate. Do you want first ride?" she asked.

Mick was mollified—they were going to ride after all. "Yes, I'd better. Prince may buck."

It was very light now; the rain had stopped; the garden smelt of wet earth and of the fallen apples rotting under the trees.

Mick mounted with a scramble. Katie had hold of the halter rope. "Do you want me to leave go?"

"Of course."

"Do be careful, then," Katie said. It seemed crazy that they should be riding a pony which belonged to film stars up and down a strange drive; wrong too. Katie wished she was at home now in the familiar, overcrowded room with the twins crying and the smell of washing drying on the radiator. They wouldn't be doing anything wrong there. Mick walked the pony down the drive; he felt at home, as though all his life he had been waiting for this moment.

"Look at me," he cried in tones of triumph, "I can ride!"

He felt that he had dreamed all this before, He started to whistle. He thought, everything comes to you in the end if you want it badly enough.

"Am I sitting properly?" he called to Katie.

He had hoped she would say, "Yes. You look as though you've ridden a lot." Instead she stood in the drive looking small and frightened. "It must be my turn now," she said. "It's getting late, really it is."

He rode once more to the gate, trotting this time. Prince seemed to know what he wanted, to be glad to

47

have someone on his back; at any rate, he pricked his ears and went willingly enough.

"It's my turn now," said Katie in a small but determined voice.

"All right. Don't look so scared. What's the matter?" He dismounted and patted Prince.

"It's getting so late," said Katie. She mounted and took hold of the halter rope.

"Shall I lead you?" asked Mick.

"Of course not."

She pressed Prince with her legs. He walked forward and she felt a tremendous sense of happiness. Nothing mattered now beyond the fact that she was riding. She patted Prince, looked at his neat ears. I'm riding, she thought, riding by myself for the first time, and as if to fit her mood, the sun broke through the clouds at that moment, laying a golden carpet across the drive for her.

"If you're all right, I'm going to collect Prince some apples," said Mick, running towards the apple trees.

She trotted, tried to rise, but failed. Each second she was feeling more at home, and Prince was wonderful, as though he understood how little she knew and was doing his best to help.

"You must stop now," said Mick, his pockets bulging with apples.

Dismounting was like waking from a dream.

"Yes. We must run all the way back," she cried.

"Don't panic," cried Mick, but she could see he was scared too. "We've stayed too long. Look at the cars going along the road over there," he cried.

They both knew it wasn't early morning any more.

They pushed Prince in his box, took off his saddle, put it and the halter away and fled.

The lane seemed unbearably long, but at last they reached the road.

"There's no need to kill ourselves. After all, she didn't say we weren't to go out before breakfast," said Mick breaking into a walk.

"Where shall we say we've been?"

"Exploring."

"But that's a lie."

"Do you want us to tell the truth, then?"

"Well, some of it."

They started to argue then, and they were still arguing when they came to the tall, semi-detached house standing beyond the stubble field.

They could see Mrs Millet waving to them from a window. Mr Millet was picking Brussels sprouts in the garden.

"It's Sunday. People shouldn't be cross on a Sunday," said Mick.

They ran up the path to the back door.

"You're back, then. About time too. Mrs Millet has been scared to death," called Mr Millet.

Breakfast had been cleared away. They could smell the joint roasting in the oven.

Toby slept by the fire. Already it seemed years since they were riding Prince up and down the drive at Four Ways. They could hear Mrs Millet coming downstairs.

There must be a joint roasting at home too, thought Katie. Whatever happens, I'm glad we had a ride, decided Mick.

"Wherever have you been?" said Mrs Millet, coming into the room, looking at them with her steady blue eyes.

"Exploring," said Mick.

"I suppose you got lost again—you kids! It's not me who cares. Kids will be kids I know that, but I'm responsible for you."

She wasn't cross. They both felt limp; they had steeled themselves to face a row. Katie began to cry. She thought, we're awful. Poor Mrs Millet. And Mick's told a lie and it's Sunday.

"Don't cry. Here, have my hanky."

Mick didn't speak. He was seeing Mrs Millet in a new light, and she wasn't so bad after all.

"We found the pony again," he said.

"What? The one that came here?"

"Yes. He belongs to some film stars."

"Come on. Sit down and let me get you some breakfast. Your shoes are soaked through, Katie. You'll be getting colds next. Really—kids. . ." exclaimed Mrs Millet.

She wasn't interested in the pony, they suddenly realised. To her he was just a pony, that was all, not something to be dreamed about, to long for, to cherish.

"And now you're to stay at home till Sunday School, do you hear? How I'm going to get your clothes dry I don't know . . ."

Chapter Seven

SUNDAY

They fidgeted at Sunday School. "I shall be waiting outside to take you home when you come out," Mrs Millet had said, and there she was as they trooped out with the other children, in the brown coat she had worn when they met for the first time on Friday. Mick couldn't help thinking how long ago that first glimpse of her seemed now; as for Katie, she was worrying about Prince again: Supposing he had drunk all his water, trampled his hay underfoot? Supposing they weren't allowed to visit him in the morning? She could see him walking round and round in his box like a lion in a cage. He would be expecting herself and Mick to turn up; at first he would be quite calm; but gradually, as he lost hope, he would start to kick the door.

"Tonight you will sit down and write to your mother. She must be wondering how you are," said Mrs Millet.

She walked very fast, her high heels going click-click along the road; the children had to run to keep up. There was no chance for any conversation between themselves; once Mick put his thumbs down to indicate failure, and Katie pulled a face which meant: No hope. Nothing doing tonight. Mick nodded assent, and thought, we'll have to get up and go to Four Ways before school, that's all. and then all too soon they had reached the house, were being hustled out of their coats and into the kitchen, where tea awaited them.

"Well, how was it? Did you learn much?" asked Mr Millet, sitting by the fire with Toby on his knees.

"Yes, thank you," said Mick.

After tea, Mrs Millet fetched them pens and paper. She seemed determined to keep them occupied. "Now write your mother a nice long letter. Poor soul, she must be worried."

"What, both of us?" asked Mick.

"Yes, each one."

Mick wrote, "Better not mention Prince yet" on the bottom of a page and passed it to Katie, who murmured, "Okay."

There didn't seem much to say. For one thing they didn't know whether Mrs Millet intended to read their letters; she might censor them, cross out passages about herself.

Katie wrote, "Dear Mum, we are happy here. The weather is fine. We each have a bedroom. We went to Sunday School this afternoon. It was nice. I hope you and Dad are well and the twins. Love Katie."

She added a postscript saying that they had enjoyed the train journey. Mick wrote two pages, mostly about their visit to the blacksmith's forge.

He finished, "We both miss you a lot, so come and see us soon."

Mrs Millet found them an envelope and a stamp. "Now put them in and seal the envelope and my husband will catch the post for you in the morning." she said.

They went to bed early.

"Now no running about tonight," said Mrs Millet, shutting their respective doors.

Mick followed her footsteps down the two flights of stairs before he slipped out of bed, crossed the room on tiptoe, found the door. Another moment and he was in Katie's room.

"I thought you'd come," she said, sitting up.

"We had better sit in the dark. They might see the light shining in the garden if we switch it on," whispered Mick.

"Poor Prince. What are we going to do? I wish we had told Mrs Millet everything. Really I do," sighed Katie. She felt very tired, and all the time at the back of her mind lurked the lost pony, hungry and abandoned, imprisoned in his loose-box without food or water.

"I shall never sleep unless we do something. Really I shan't," she said.

"Don't panic."

"That's what you always say."

"We left him with plenty of hay and water. He should be all right until tomorrow," said Mick.

"You mean get up early again, before breakfast?"

"That's all we can do."

"She'll probably be on the look-out for us."

"We'll have to risk that. We must will ourselves to wake up at half-past five, knock our heads on our pillows five times."

They had learned that trick from the Nesbit books,

which Mick had borrowed from the library a long time ago.

"All right," said Katie.

"See you at five, then."

"Do you think we'll be able to ride."

"Well, we shall have a clear two hours."

Katie let her head sink back on the pillow; she heard Mick creep from the room; then she fell asleep.

Mick remembered to bang his head five times. He saw them riding Prince again, in a bridle this time, then he too slept.

It was morning when Katie awakened; a sullen sun shone amid clouds above the garden. Mrs Millet was saying, "Wake up, Katie. Breakfast is ready. It's school today."

She had been dreaming of the chestnut pony, of hunting him across fields dappled by sunlight. For a time the cry of hounds had mingled with Mrs Millet's voice; now suddenly, she knew she was with reality—that it was late, too late to visit Prince; for already she could smell breakfast cooking downstairs.

"Thank you. I'm getting up," she said, springing from bed.

"Don't be long," said Mrs Millet, turning to rap on Mick's door.

He'll be thirsty, she thought. He'll never trust us now. We've let him down; and he was so wonderful yesterday.

"Put on a skirt, your grey shirt and red jumper," called Mrs Millet, who had been through her clothes, washing some, ironing others.

"Oh Mick, we're late," called Katie.

"I know," he answered. Getting out of bed, he thought how things might have been, returning across the stubble; they could have ridden, learned to rise to Prince's springy trot. The whole day's wasted, thought Mick, finding his grey trousers. Why did we oversleep? Why, why, why?

Neither of them ate much breakfast.

"Now, don't get upset about going to a new school. Our school is as nice as you would find anywhere . . . anyway, by all accounts, you'll soon be going to the Grammar School, Mick," said Mrs Millet, clearing away their plates.

"I'm going to be a vet." For a moment Mick's face lit up; he saw himself getting out of a car. I'm going to get to the top, he thought. I'm going to judge at shows, travel; perhaps I'll take a job in Canada for a time. I might even try America. He saw himself boarding a plane, becoming famous young Michael Smallbone.

"What are you going to do when you're grown up, Katie?" asked Mrs Millet.

"I want a job with horses."

"I should have thought an office job would have been better—would bring in more money at any rate," said Mrs Millet.

"No, I'd rather be with horses," said Katie.

"I don't know what you see in them, great ugly brutes," said Mr Millet, kissing his wife on the forehead.

"Well, goodbye, kids. If you can't be good, be careful," he said, slamming the door after him.

"Where do you get it from?"

"What?" asked Mick.

"This love of horses," replied Mrs Millet.

"Well, Dad grew up in the country. He lived there, until Grandpa had to move to town for a new job," Mick answered. He remembered things his father had said: "There's nothing like an egg straight from the hen, like you get in the country. When I'm too old to work any more, we'll find a little cottage somewhere in the country won't we, Mother. We'll grow our own vegetables, keep a few chickens."

For the children, these remarks and many more had given the country a magic quality; it had become a sort of paradise, a place where you went for a holiday, where food was fresher and days seemed longer.

"Did he ride, then?"

"Only on grandpa's horse."

"I suppose you could say it was in your blood then?"

"Well, Mum grew up in a town," said Katie, remembering things her mother had said. "There were hard times in the sixties. we made our own skirts to go to school in. . ."

"But she always loved animals," said Mick, and as Mrs Millet hustled them into their coats, found their lunch money, opened the door, he began to think of the pony again. We must try to get to him in the lunch hour, he thought. We must do something.

"Now don't lose your lunch money and don't dawdle; you haven't much time," said Mrs Millet.

"Poor Prince!" exclaimed Katie the moment they

reached the road. "Can't we feed him now?"

"There isn't time, you idiot. We can't be late for school our very first morning . . ."

"Couldn't we explain?"

"They wouldn't understand . . ."

"I think we should tell the police about him. We should have done that before. Really, we should."

They started to quarrel then.

"Can't you see we're doing the film stars a favour? They'll come home and find a lovely fat pony. They should be grateful," said Mick.

"But one shouldn't ride other people's ponies without their permission. Really one shouldn't . . ."

"Really one shouldn't," mimicked Mick.

"But it's true. Really it is."

"Really it is."

"Sometimes I hate you."

They reached the school. They stopped quarrelling. They stood and looked at the building.

"It's quite small," said Katie.

"Next year I shall be at the Grammar School."

"You hope . . ."

They stood hovering until one of the teachers saw them. "Come in," she called, "You're the Smallbones, aren't you? It's nice to see you."

The morning seemed endless, and directly afterwards there was lunch. They both realised then that there was to be no escape, and all through lunch Katie saw the pony banging his door, again and again, endlessly, in vain.

We should have left him straying, she thought. We shouldn't have shut him in. He would have been

57

better facing sticks and stones than hunger and thirst.

He'll be all right, thought Mick, but I wish we had gone this morning, all the same. Perhaps Katie is right. Perhaps we'd better tell the police. It seemed like a kind of miracle him coming into the garden like that our very first night, as though fate was on our side, but it might be just coincidence. One can't really tell. And, as Dad says, "Honesty is the best policy . . ."

He wanted to tell Katie that he had changed his mind, that he agreed with her, but there wasn't a chance. It wasn't until three thirty that they found a chance to speak together, and then they were trooping out of school with all the other children and there was rain falling in dark sheets, and rumbles of thunder, and the whole landscape seemed to be waiting for something.

"Katie," said Mick, and then it came, lightning, thunder, more rain as if all the sky had suddenly opened. They started to run, someone called, but they could only hear the rain, the streaming gutters, another burst of thunder.

"We'd better go home," cried Mick.

"But Prince. . ."

"We can't go there in this . . ."

Chapter Eight

HE'S HUNGRY

"Why didn't you shelter somewhere? You're soaked."
Mrs Millet pulled off their coats. Outside the storm
still raged; the rain beat against the windows, doors
slammed, gutters overflowed.

Katie felt defeated. There was a choking sensation
in her throat. She felt guilty, almost criminal. She
wanted to cry. She could only think, if Mum was here
she would understand.

Mick was still determined. Taking off his wet
shoes, he thought, we'll go after tea. We can think of
some excuse; there must be something we can say.
And all the time Mrs Millet's voice went on: "Look at
your shoes. How I shall get them dry I don't know.
Really, I can't have both of you in bed with colds.
Really, kids . . ."

"We must do something," said Katie, climbing the
attic stairs.

"We must go after tea."

"But what can we say?"

"Wait and see."

"Poor Prince. He must be desperate. . ."

"He's not starving yet."

"He soon will be."

"We'll go after tea."

Tea was late. They sat about waiting for Mr Millet

59

to come in. Katie watched the clock—five o'clock, five fifteen, five thirty.

"Can we go out after tea?" she asked Mrs Millet.

"Go out on a night like this? You must be mad."

"But we must."

"There's no must about it. You're not going out." Mrs Millet drew back the curtain. "Look at the rain."

It was still coming down in torrents. They could see it lashing the window. There was a wind now which whipped round the house; there was a fallen branch in the garden.

"Go out on a night like this, whatever next?" asked Mrs Millet drawing the curtain.

"It's the pony. we haven't fed him," said Katie. Suddenly everything seemed hopeless, they had gone wrong somewhere and now nothing would ever be right again . . . "He's hungry . . ." she wailed.

"Well, you haven't got a pony," said Mrs Millet.

"It's the lost one. . ." said Mick. He wished she had never spoken. They'd never get out now; he knew that.

"Well, you're not responsible for him. Whatever next?" asked Mrs Millet.

"We were looking after him," said Mick in a small, determined voice.

"Well, perhaps this will be a lesson to you to mind your own business. He won't starve tonight. You can see him in the morning, and Mr Millet will try and find out more about him. We can't have you breaking your little hearts over someone else's pony."

Mrs Millet put her arm round Katie. "Don't carry on like that," she said.

The children hardly ate any tea, because it seemed awful to eat while Prince had nothing. Outside it still rained, but now it was a settled downpour which would certainly last all night.

Mrs Millet saw the children to bed.

"Now, no monkey tricks," she said. "Do you think your mother would forgive me if she thought you were running about in the middle of the night, and all over a pony which has nothing to do with you?"

"I don't know," answered Katie.

"Well, I do . . ." said Mrs Millet.

Katie knew she would never sleep. she thought, everything's awful. Why did we have to leave home? I'm unhappier than I've ever been before. I should like to run away, but there'd still be the pony banging at his stable door, looking for us, whinnying all in vain. Faint music from the TV in the kitchen floated upstairs. Then she fell to thinking about Mr Millet. His wife had said he would do something about Prince tomorrow. What did that mean? Did it mean he would send him somewhere to be destroyed, like the police did sometimes when no-one claimed a lost pet? She began to cry then helplessly into her pillow. She saw Prince being led to a slaughter-house, screaming with fright; he would die and they would never have a pony, never, never. She searched for a handkerchief without success. The room seemed full of shadows, the windows creaked, the wind beat against the walls, and she could hear the rain falling still, as though it would never stop.

She searched through the drawers, found a handkerchief at last and blew her nose, then she heard Mick saying, "Katie, listen."

He was whispering through the wall which separated their rooms.

"I daren't come out of here, because I'm sure she's listening. But we must go to Prince tonight. Do you agree?"

"Yes." It was a relief to know that they were going to do something. "I can't sleep."

"We must stay awake a long time, and then when everything is quiet we'll go."

"We mustn't be caught."

"We won't be."

Katie crept back to bed; she stayed sitting up, her bedclothes pulled up to her chin.

She thought about a great many things: about the muddle their life was now, how she never had anything she wanted, how dirty cities were and how clean the country by comparison, and all the time in the back of her mind there was the lost pony waiting for them. She thought how lovely it would be to own an animal like that, how she and Mick would ride every morning before school until they were good enough to ride in horse shows, to enter for musical chairs, for bending races, and on some distant day for more serious events—for jumping, and showing classes, and perhaps the Prince Philip cup. She saw them winning, being handed a silver cup and then she came back to reality and saw the rather bleak room and heard the windows creaking, and the rain outside; and the comparison was so awful that she began to cry again.

Next door Mick said automatically, "Don't cry, Katie. It won't help."

He was lying in bed, making plans. They had to slip out unnoticed, and it was still raining; their outdoor clothes were most likely drying on the high rack in the kitchen. Would they be able to get them down without making a noise?

They must feed Prince, return at once and replace their clothes. They mustn't trip, nor kick a stair rod, nor whisper, because any noise could jeopardize the whole venture. And they must be back before the Millets rose from their bed.

"Katie, are you still awake?" he asked.

"Yes. We can't go yet. Really we can't."

"I know that. I'm not such a fool. But listen. We'll have to get our clothes off the rack in the kitchen."

"Oh dear. We're doing so many bad things ..." whispered Katie.

"But in a good cause."

But was it? wondered Katie. Shouldn't they have told someone straightaway, as soon as they discovered the lost pony living by himself near an empty house with nothing provided for him?

"Ssh! She's coming," whispered Mick.

Mrs Millet switched on the passage light. They knew that, because they could see it shining under their doors. And they were both pretending to be asleep when she tucked up each in turn before she went downstairs again.

"That means she's going to be up soon," whispered Mick through the wall.

"I feel so mean. She's nice really," said Katie. "And

63

it's true Mum wouldn't like us to be out in this storm."

"She might think differently if she knew the circumstances."

They couldn't hear the TV any more, and that meant that the Millets were most likely upstairs washing and cleaning their teeth.

We'll have to give them time to fall asleep, thought Mick. I wish the rain would stop. The night must be as black as ink. Supposing we can't find the way, miss the lane in the dark? We mustn't, that's all.

He lay in bed tense, his hands clasped tightly together. He was sleepy now, and because of that, he sat up presently and listened to the rain on the window, and thought how the streets at home must be, and how his parents would be asleep.

He fell to counting seconds, and when he had counted five hundred he said, through the wall, "Katie. Let's go."

But Katie had fallen asleep and he had to creep into her room and whisper, "Wake up, Katie. It's Mick."

They crept downstairs together. The house was dark, devoid of all sound. They found the switch in the kitchen, stood blinking in the sudden light.

"Better get our clothes down," murmured Mick. It didn't take then long to dress, but they couldn't get the clothes' rack up again.

They struggled in silence; the cords which controlled it became entangled.

"We'll leave it; we can try again when we get back," said Mick.

64

They felt better when they were outside, though the rain engulfed them, and visibility was nearly nil, and the whole countryside seemed empty, as though they alone of all living things were fool enough to venture out.

They started to run, and the rain bit into their faces. They bowed their heads. "We must keep together," said Mick.

They could feel stubble beneath their feet. Memory guided them across the field. Beyond, the road was wet but hard under their soaking shoes.

"It's not far now," said Mick, stopping to brush his hair out of his eyes.

"We won't stay, will we?" Katie asked. She was wet to the skin; her clothes clung to her, dripped on to the bleak road.

"No. we'll give him food and water and then go back." Mick started to run again.

Supposing this makes us ill? wondered Katie and saw herself in bed. Mrs Millet cross but kind, her mother bringing her flowers.

"Not much further," said Mick.

She was dropping behind her brother, though her legs were still running one-two, one-two along the road.

"Here's the lane," Mick called back into the endless dark.

She tried to run faster. "Don't wait for me," she called. "I know the way."

Mick wasn't tired. He had always been a good runner. He reached the drive and saw that the bungalow was still in darkness. He ran faster, put on a tremendous burst of speed, reached the stable, "Prince, we've come," he called.

He stood looking at the loose-box. The door stood open; nothing moved inside.

"He's gone. He isn't here," he cried.

"Gone?" echoed Katie from the other end of the drive, breaking into a walk.

"Yes, gone."

It was an anticlimax. Somewhere they had failed. All this for nothing, thought Mick.

"But how did he get out?" asked Katie.

"They stood together, two dripping, bedraggled figures staring at the empty loose-box. Somewhere far away an owl hooted dismally; otherwise all was silence, except for the sound of falling rain, which had never ceased.

Katie felt like sitting down, but there was nowhere to sit; now they had to go back; perhaps they would never see the lost pony again and because of that if Mrs Millet caught them now it wouldn't really matter.

And then Mick heard a noise; it was like the noise they had heard that first night when the pony had trespassed in the Millets' garden—somewhere hoofs brushed against grass.

"Listen," he yelled. "Don't move. Listen."

Chapter Nine

HE'S MAD OR SOMETHING

"He's under the apple trees," cried Katie. They ran forward together against the driving rain.

Branches caught their hair, sending showers of rain down their necks; they slipped on squashy fallen apples, tripped over roots. The pony was standing with his back to the wind. He didn't turn his head as they approached.

"We needn't have worried. He's had plenty of apples to eat and the grass is wet enough to quench his thirst," said Katie.

It seemed absurd now that they had bothered to come, for Prince could easily have waited till morning.

Katie started to shiver; her feet squelched in her shoes, her hair hung limp. She thought, it'll be days before my clothes are dry.

Mick was talking to the pony. "You'd better come back to your box. It's awfully wet outside," he said. He looked at Prince. "He must have been stuffing. Look how fat he is."

"We'd better hurry back," cried Katie. We don't want to get into another row, and I'm freezing."

Mick took hold of the chestnut pony's mane.

"Come on Prince," he said.

"Make him trot. Hurry up. I'm soaking." Katie was hating the whole expedition. When we get back it'll be time to get up, she thought. And it's only our second day at the school here; we won't be able to take in anything; we'll keep falling asleep.

"Something's wrong," cried Mick. He had let go of the pony, who was tearing up the ground with his hoofs. "He's mad or something."

It was too dark to see much. And the rain hadn't ceased and all around them were apple trees. But they could see Prince and he was tearing in circles, kicking at his stomach, rolling, getting up again, rolling.

"He can't be mad. He was all right yesterday," cried Katie. Her heart was thudding against her ribs; she was afraid the pony might suddenly attack them; anything could happen in the dark.

"Keep away from him, Mick," she cried. "Don't go near."

"Perhaps he's having a fit," said Mick. He stood staring at the whirling pony, trying to remember everything he had read in his tattered Everyday Farrier. Did horses have hysteria like dogs? Could hunger drive them insane? "He was quite calm when we came. We'd better try to get him into the loose-box. Come on, Prince." Mick wasn't afraid. He was surprised by his own calmness. "It's all right, Prince. Don't you remember me?"

The pony was standing still now, trembling and sweating. He let Mick take hold of him.

"That's a good pony. Come on."

The whole night was extraordinary to Mick. Nothing like this had ever happened to him before, but the strange thing was he felt quite at home. Prince might have been his own pony in his parents' orchard and Prince sensed that, and followed Mick into the loose-box.

"If only there's a light," said Mick.

Katie found a switch, pushed it down and miraculously light flooded the box. For a moment the three of them stood blinking, then the children started to examine Prince.

The pony stood with a strained expression, his ears straight up, his eyes seeming to wait for something, his coat wet with sweat.

"He must be ill," said Mick at last.

"What can we do?" asked Katie in a whisper. Outside rain battered against the loose-box. The children felt very far from their real home, further than they had ever been before.

"We can't leave him. He's sick," said Mick.

"But what can we do?"

"We can't let him down now," said Mick.

He tried to think. Already hours might have passed since they left the Millets' house: He was tired, his feet were cold in his trainers, soon it would be morning, and what would Mrs Millet say when she found them gone? He could see her searching their rooms calling, finding the clothes' rack down in the kitchen. Katie seemed to read his thoughts, for she said,

"Mrs Millet will be furious; and she'll send us away."

"Well, we can't leave Prince like this. Let's fetch him some oats, see if he'll eat."

Mick walked out of the loose-box, his head bowed against the rain. If we had come yesterday, this would never have happened, he thought. Perhaps he's been eating rotten apples, or found the oats, or maybe there's yew in the garden, he thought with a flash of panic, and for a moment tears blinded his eyes and he saw the pony dying. He found the oats, and heard Katie calling, "Quick, Mick. Come quickly. He's going mad again."

He ran back through the blinding rain, tripped over a stone, sprawled in the yard; the rain beat on his back; he could hear Prince's hoofs thudding against the sides of the stable. "Hurry, Mick," called Katie.

He got up; his knee was bleeding, and he left a pool of blood where he had fallen which joined the water whirling away down the drive.

Katie was standing in the far corner of the box, while Prince rolled wildly, leapt to his feet, rolled again.

"He's gone mad. Really he has," she cried. She had reached the end of her resistance; she longed for a grown-up to come, to take over, to tell them what to do, to relieve them of responsibility.

"We need a halter," said Mick. The night was getting lighter; dawn couldn't be far off now. It must be Tuesday already—their first Tuesday in the country.

Why did this have to happen to us? wondered Katie. Suddenly life was terrible; they were miles from home with a mad pony in the middle of the night; she was trapped in a corner.

70

"I'll get a halter," said Mick.

"I'm frightened," she pleaded.

"Don't be a idiot. He won't hurt you."

She tried to calm the pony. "Whoa, whoa. It's all right. Really it is. We're your friends. Whoa." She wanted to get out of the corner, but Prince was rolling again now and she was afraid of his thrashing hoofs.

Mick's knee was still bleeding. He found a halter after what seemed an age. Prince was standing still when he returned, while Katie, small and frightened, remained trapped in a corner.

"I think we'll have to get a vet," said Mick.

"But how?"

"I don't know."

He held out some oats to Prince, slipped the halter over his ears. The pony stood exhausted, his eyes watchful for a new spasm of pain.

"I've remembered something—colic," said Mick.

He saw a description of it in his book. "There should be a drench somewhere."

"What is colic?"

"Horses have it because they can't be sick."

"Is it serious?"

"They can die of it."

They stood looking at the pony.

"Perhaps he's getting better," suggested Katie.

"I don't think so."

The sky was light in the East now.

"Mrs Millet will be furious," remarked Katie with a shiver.

"We can't help that. One can't just leave a sick

71

animal. Will you hold Prince while I look for a drench; he'll be all right for a minute."

"What if he's eaten yew?"

"He'll most likely die."

Katie took hold of the halter and began to cry again. "What is it, Prince?" she asked. "What's the matter?"

"I'll be back in a minute," Mick said.

It's morning now, thought Katie, and saw her mother getting up, moving stealthily about her tasks so as not to wake anybody. The street lights would be off and above the chimneys the sky would be growing lighter, revealing the rain. The paper-boy would be riding his bicycle along the street and a few people would be walking home after night shift. Everything would be safe and familiar.

Mick couldn't find a drench. He found a great many old bottles at the back of the garage, but the ones which didn't say Gordon's Gin or Vin Rose had Turpentine scrawled across them or weed-killer or were obviously beer bottles, or had once contained oil.

And now Katie was calling again: "Mick, he's mad again. I can't hold him. He's pulling awfully, Mick . . ."

He ran back. Katie had let go of the halter. The pony was rolling.

"Why didn't you hold on?"

"I tried to . . ."

"We'll have to get a vet," said Mick.

"I'll go."

"Where to?"

They stood staring at one another. Outside they could see the rain, the drive, the gate beyond.

"We've been up the whole night," said Katie.

"And done nothing," snapped Mick.

"We've done our best."

"I don't know where there's a phone box," said Mick.

"There must be a farm somewhere near. Wouldn't a farm have a drench?" asked Katie.

"We must get a vet," said Mick firmly. "We'll have to break into the house . . ."

"Break in? Supposing we're caught?" cried Katie.

She saw them in court, the disgrace, their parents' sorrow.

"Can't you see he's in agony? He'll twist a gut in a moment. Come on. You'd better come—I may need a leg-up on to a sill."

She followed her brother. The torrent of rain had slackened. Daylight had come.

"I wish we knew the time. Really I do," said Katie.

"It wouldn't make any difference," replied Mick.

They walked round the house. "Perhaps there's a coal-hole somewhere. Couldn't we get in through the coal-cellar?"

"I don't think bungalows have cellars—not new ones, anyway," said Mick.

They chose the kitchen window. "I'll break in by the latch," said Mick, looking for a stone.

They could hear Prince banging against the loose-box walls again.

"He's getting worse," cried Mick, breaking the window.

Katie pushed him through, wishing that she was anywhere but at Four Ways, breaking in.

"I'll be as quick as I can," said Mick.

"But supposing there isn't a telephone?" cried Katie looking round the garden for wires.

"There must be one," said Mick.

Chapter Ten

ALL THIS FOR NOTHING

Mick found the light switch.

"Are you all right?" called Katie through the broken window.

"Yes thank you."

The kitchen was beautifully equipped with labour-saving devices. Mick opened a door and found himself in the hall.

"Shall I go back to Prince?" called Katie.

"Yes, if you like."

Mick found the sitting room and a telephone on the wall.

If only it hasn't been cut off, he thought. He could hear Prince thrashing round the loose-box, even here in the house; then the banging stopped and he supposed Katie had hold of the pony, and was calming him.

He found a telephone directory but it wasn't the yellow pages so he couldn't find a vet, in the long list of names. He nearly dialled 999, then he thought of calling the operator instead and dialled 0. He could see miles of open country through the sitting room window—far away cows were being driven along a road, sheep were penned in a field, the trees were russet brown.

A voice answered him. "Hello, can I help you," it asked.

"I want a vet; it's urgent," said Mick.

"I'll put you through to enquiries."

Prince was banging again now; the Millets had probably searched the house for them by this time.

"Enquiries. Can I help you?"

"I want a vet, please. It's urgent."

"Where are you speaking from?"

Mick looked at the telephone. "Rushcombe 705606," he answered.

He looked around the sitting room for the first time. There was a leather sofa and arm chairs. A huge portrait stood on the grand piano. His wet hands had left smears on the telephone and directory; his feet had left marks on the luxurious white carpet.

"The number you require is Rushcombe 489230" said a voice on the other end.

Everything was taking far too long. Prince should have been treated hours ago. It wasn't raining any more. By this time Dad would be on his way to work, thought Mick.

It was some time before anyone answered the phone.

"Hello, can I help you?" asked a woman's voice at last.

"I want to speak to a vet; it's urgent," said Mick.

"He's worse. Aren't you ever going to get someone to come?" Katie was screaming through the kitchen window. "He's going to die. Really he is . . ."

"Shut up. I can't hear," shouted Mick. He had

broken into a sweat. His wet coat had left dark marks all over the chair in which he was sitting.

"I am a vet," said the woman.

"It's about a pony. I think he's eaten yew or something. I think he's going to die," Mick's eyes clouded suddenly with tears.

"Is he coming soon—the vet, I mean?" yelled Katie.

"Where are you speaking from?"

"From Four Ways, somewhere near Rushcombe."

"Right, I know it."

"We found the pony sick. The house is empty. We've broken in," said Mick.

The vet seemed to think that very extraordinary.

"This isn't a hoax, is it?" she asked.

"No please come. I think you'd better bring a stomach pump. If you don't come soon he'll die."

"All right. I'm on my way."

Mick replaced the receiver; his knees were knocking together, and he saw that his cut had left a spot of scarlet blood on the white carpet.

He went back to the kitchen. The sun was shining through the window on the fridge, the washing machine, the gleaming kitchen units and a green sink. His sister had gone. Somewhere a bird was singing. He opened the back door and saw that Katie was holding the pony in the drive.

"He's cut himself," she called.

"I'd better shut the gate. We don't want him to get away from us before the vet comes."

"He's kicked half of one of the walls down," Katie said.

Mick shut the gate.

"Is he coming soon?" called Katie.

"I think so, but it's a she," Mick said.

"What does she think is wrong with Prince?"

"I didn't ask."

"You're awfully dirty. Really you are," said Katie, looking at her brother.

"I know. I've left the sitting room in an awful mess. But you can't talk," said Mick.

"He has spasms. He's better now, but in a minute he'll be worse again," Katie said, looking at the chestnut pony.

"I've just remembered. There's two kinds of colic; one's called spasmodic," replied Mick.

"It must be that, then."

They were wet and tired and grubby. "There's going to be a terrible row when we do get back," Katie said.

"I know."

"Do you think we'll be sent to a special school?"

"No, I don't think so."

The pony was becoming restless again.

"We'd better lead him up and down the drive. That's supposed to help," said Mick.

They didn't talk much after that, but took it in turns to lead the pony.

Once Katie said, "Supposing she can't find us?"

Mick replied after a pause, "She'll probably go to the police. . ."

Time passed very slowly. The children's thoughts were dismal, and there seemed no hope in the future, nothing but unpleasantness. Then at last they saw a car coming along the lane. Katie was leading Prince, and Mick was searching for apples which were not too rotten to eat.

"Here she comes," called Mick.

"I hope she's nice," said Katie.

"She must be or she wouldn't be a vet," replied Mick. "I wish we looked tidier; you look as though you've been pulled through several hedges backwards."

"We should have washed in the kitchen," Katie said.

Prince was much quieter; the sun was shining still.

"If only I wasn't so hungry," complained Katie.

"Here she is."

The vet was slim and grey haired; she wore a white coat over a coat and skirt.

"Well, let's look at the pony." The vet started to talk to Prince. "Hello, what's the matter? Have you eaten something . . . too many apples perhaps?"

"There are lots of rotten apples in the orchard," said Mick.

"He's been out for some time. He's been in agony, really he has," added Katie.

Prince was standing quietly now, but his neck was still wet with sweat.

"I've got a drench in my car," said the vet.

"She seems nice," whispered Katie.

"Yes she's all right," agreed Mick.

"You two look as though you could do with a wash and some dry clothes," said the vet, coming back from her car with a drench and syringe. "How long have you been here?"

"I don't know. Most of the night I suppose," said Mick.

"What made you come up here in the first place?"

"We meant to come here all yesterday, but we weren't allowed to, because of the rain," explained Mick.

"I see. Catch hold of his tongue, one of you please."

She's trying to sum us up, Mick thought.

They drenched the pony. "I may have to give him an enema. Do you think there's any soap in the house, or warm water?"

"Not warm water," replied Mick.

"When did you first find this pony?" asked the vet, who was less immaculate now because her white coat was stained with drench. She slid the point of the syringe into the pony's neck.

"We'd better tell the whole story," replied Mick.

"Yes. Right from the beginning," agreed Katie.

"You see, we aren't living with our parents any more," began Mick.

"You haven't run away from home, have you?" asked the vet, in a resigned voice.

"No. We'd never do that!" cried Katie.

"You see, we've always wanted a pony," said Mick.

"We ought to have told the police . . ." interrupted Katie.

"You'd better begin at the beginning and make it short. You'll both be ill, if you stand about much longer in those damp clothes," said the vet.

They told their story, frequently interrupting each other.

"Do you think we've been very bad?" asked Katie

80

when they had finished.

"Yes and no. You should have told the police really. You see, I know this pony. He isn't called Prince at all, but Blue Grass. He's quite a valuable pony. People have been up here looking for him once or twice, but I can only suppose he didn't come here straightaway."

"I thought he was a good pony. Didn't I, Katie?" Mick said.

"Did he live here?" asked Katie.

"Yes. But when the Canningtons had to go to America they sent him to the Littleheath Stables."

"But they're miles away," interrupted Mick.

"Only about ten or twelve miles across country," replied the vet.

"I suppose he'll have to go back. Do you think they'll give us a reward?" asked Mick.

"Why should they? If you had gone to the police, it might have been different."

So it's all over, thought Katie. We'll never find another lost pony, and there'll be no reward. She felt very gloomy now; there seemed nothing to look forward to—only rows with Mrs Millet, perhaps new foster-parents, perhaps a children's home.

"I wonder if there's a rug anywhere. You'd better put him back in the box. We can dry him with some straw," said the vet.

They couldn't find a horse-rug.

"I think I had better ring up from here since you've broken into the house already. They might be able to send a trailer over for him straightaway," said the vet. "You'd better keep on drying him," she said.

The pony seemed much better. He looked in his manger hopefully for oats; he nuzzled the children's pockets.

"So you're Blue Grass," said Mick.

"I wish we'd never set eyes on him. really I do," said Katie.

"At least we each had one ride," answered Mick.

"We've still got to face Mrs Millet."

"I know. I wish we knew the time."

"Supposing she sends us away?" asked Katie.

"With any luck, she won't."

"And we thought Prince coming into the garden, on our first night, was a kind of miracle," sighed Katie.

"Good may come of it yet."

"I don't see how. Really I don't."

"Here she comes," said Mick.

They had stopped drying Prince; now they started again. They were both tired, and there was still Mrs Millet to face, and a whole day at school.

"They are sending over a trailer," said the vet, opening the loose-box door.

"Were they cross?" asked Katie.

"No. I don't think so. How long can you stay here? I don't want to leave Blue Grass alone if I can help it, only you're so wet," said the vet.

"We're used to that, aren't we, Katie? And I'm not cold at all," replied Mick.

"I hate leaving you here; but I have a surgery at nine," said the vet.

"Is it nine already?" cried Katie.

"A quarter to."

Katie and Mick looked at one another, and they both saw in their imagination the teacher calling their names at school in vain.

"He shouldn't be long with the trailer. I think the pony should be all right now. Someone will have to tell the police about the kitchen window being broken. You'd better ask the chap who comes with the trailer to do that." She was going; she had taken off her stained white coat.

"Ought we to leave some money for the telephone call?" cried Mick.

"No, I'll tell the Canningtons about it when they're back. I see them sometimes. Don't let Blue Grass get cold—he's a valuable pony. Well, the best of luck to both of you." She started the engine, turned the car neatly. "I hope all ends well."

"We didn't pay her," said Mick.

"How could we? We haven't any money," answered Katie. Her teeth were chattering. "Do you think she was cross with us? Perhaps we got her out of bed."

"Vets are used to that."

'Listen. There's someone calling, or else I've got noises in my head. Listen . . ."

"I can't hear anything," answered Mick.

"You're not listening."

"They stood in silence, Katie with one arm round the chestnut pony's neck, Mick rubbing his hands together; and they heard a voice calling, "Mick, Katie. Where are you? Whatever do you think you are doing? Mick, Katie, Mick . . ."

"It's Mrs Millet," said Katie at last.

"She must have walked," answered Mick.

83

"How did she find her way?"

"We'll know soon enough."

"Oh, Prince," cried Katie. "All this for nothing."

"Mick, Katie. It's no good hiding. I know where you are."

"We're not hiding. We're here waiting for you," shouted Mick.

"Really we are," added Katie.

Chapter Eleven

IT'S DAVID SMITH

They judged her mood by her walk. She was taking short, quick steps, and wore a scarf over her head.

"I shall take the blame," announced Mick.

"No; you won't. It was my fault too."

"I got you out of bed. You know I did, Katie."

They clung to the chestnut pony. He seemed to understand the situation, for he stood quietly, only turning to nuzzle them affectionately from time to time.

"So here you are . . ." cried Mrs Millet. "And I told you to leave the pony alone till the morning, didn't I?"

"He was sick. Really he was," answered Katie, fighting back tears.

"He might have been dead by now if we hadn't come," said Mick. Now Mrs Millet was here, he wasn't afraid any more; he was certain they had saved the pony's life; surely someone would be grateful.

"It's me you'll be getting into trouble. What do you think the authorities are going to say? You not at school and all," cried Mrs Millet. "You don't want to get into trouble, do you?" she pleaded. "And all over a pony which isn't yours even. I've never met kids like you before."

"We've been brought up to be kind to animals, you see," said Katie and she saw her mother again carrying buckets of water down to Nelly.

"Yes; but this is going a bit too far. Whatever time did you get up? And now the lady in the car says you've got to wait till the trailer comes. It's all right for her—she's not responsible. What do you think I'm going to say to your teacher? It'll take a bit of explaining . . ."

They knew by her voice that she was softening, that she wasn't really angry, only worried about the future.

"She can't expel us," said Mick.

"Hadn't you better give the pony some food? He looks hungry to me. Where's the hay? I'll get him some."

She went click-clack in her high heels to the shed and brought back an armful of hay.

"Mr Millet's none too pleased either. This is the last time I take on anybody else's kids. It's too much responsibility." She looked at the pony. "You don't look sick to me either."

"He's better now. He was bad. Really he was," said Katie.

"I wish that trailer would come. You'll be getting pneumonia next."

"We're used to getting wet. We'll be all right," Mick said.

It was raining again. The sodden apple trees drooped like tired people; the sky promised nothing but more rain.

"I don't know why you like the country so much.

Give me the town any day," said Mrs Millet.

"It's because we like animals," replied Katie.

"And you broke into the kitchen too. I hope that's not a habit of yours . . ."

"What?" Mick asked.

"Breaking into other people's houses."

"We've never done it before. Really we haven't," Katie said. Her whole body was aching with cold; she no longer cared what happened. All she wanted now was food, clean, dry clothes and a chance to sleep.

"Look. There's the trailer coming," cried Katie.

"Where is it coming from?" asked Mrs Millet.

"The Littleheath Stables," Mick answered.

"That's a big place," said Mrs Millet.

Katie saw rows of loose-boxes, brooms with skips, jumps in a paddock.

"I wish we could go there," she said.

"Whatever will you be wanting next?" demanded Mrs Millet.

"Other children have ponies," Katie said.

"It's coming up the drive. It's here. Goodbye Prince, goodbye," cried Mick.

They both turned to the chestnut pony. We'll never see him again, thought Katie. This is goodbye for ever and ever, for always. It's like the dancing lessons I wanted, the piano I couldn't have because of the people below us not liking the noise. It's all been like a dream really, that's how I shall remember it, anyway.

"Goodbye, Blue Grass, I hope you'll be happy; and don't get out again, will you? . . ."

Mick's voice, broke on a sob. I'm not going to cry. I'm

87

too old to cry, he thought. For a moment he buried his face in the pony's mane. Then he turned to face the figure stepping from the car into the pouring rain.

"Why, it's David Smith!" cried Mrs Millet.

The children stared at the boy standing before them. He looked young, not more than eighteen. They remembered seeing him on TV that first night in the Millet's house, which was only a day or two ago, but which might now have belonged to another life, so much had happened since.

"I expect I've kept you waiting. I'm sorry. You all look soaked to the skin."

The children expected him to be angry; they waited for a torrent of abuse, for a lecture, for something drastic to happen.

"You seem to have recovered Blue Grass. He looks well enough now. We're all very grateful to you . . ." David Smith pushed his hair out of his eyes. "He's been lost for ten days, and it has seemed like ten years. He's a valuable pony. The Canningtons have been ringing the stable every night from Hollywood. It's been no joke," said David Smith.

"Didn't you think of looking here?" asked Mrs Millet.

"We came every day for three days; then we gave up," explained David.

For a moment they all stood together in the loose-box.

"You're not angry with us, then?" Mick asked at last.

"No. But I'd like to know the whole story. Here, help me on with this rug," David said.

When the pony was rugged and bandaged and had been safely led into the trailer, the children sat in the car and told their story, or rather as much as they dared with Mrs Millet beside them.

The more they told the more shamefaced they became; they could see now how wrong they had been to ride the pony, that they'd been mad to give him a name.

"We thought him coming was a sort of miracle. Really we did," finished Katie.

"I knew he was a good pony right from the start," Mick remarked with pride.

It was still raining. For a moment David was silent, and Katie, with a sense of panic, thought, supposing he's furious? He may ring up the police, write to Mum. She looked at the car; it was an old Ford Fiesta, shabby and comfortable like a room which has been lived in for years without being redecorated.

"Will the film stars be angry?" she asked.

"No. Not with you, at any rate," David replied. He was trying to sum up the children. What were their parents like? he wondered. How had they gained this knowledge and love of horses, which was enough to fetch them from their beds in the middle of the night? How had Mick known right from the beginning that Blue Grass needed a drench? They looked quite ordinary, except for the determination which shone in Mick's eyes, and in the way they talked, which told you at once that here were two strong characters.

"How do you know so much about ponies, anyway?" asked David, starting the engine.

"That's all they think about," replied Mrs Millet, taking David back in a flash to his own childhood, to his mother saying the same thing—or, rather, "Horses is all he cares about. Horses, horses all day along."

They are kindred spirits, he thought—or, rather, two people under the same spell as I have been all these years. And though David was only eighteen, looking at Mick and Katie, he felt suddenly old.

"You must come over to the stables," he said. "I can't help you much, because I'm only an assistant there. I break and ride and school the horses. But once I hadn't a pony either, so I know what it's like."

"We haven't much money, we can't afford lessons," Mick said.

"Well, there are not many ponies, anyway. Blue Grass is at livery," said David driving down the lane. "But if you're anything like I was, it's good just to look at horses."

"I want to be a vet," explained Mick.

"Are you good at maths and Latin?"

"Yes, I am," replied Mick firmly. "I'm going to pass my exams and then I'm going to the Grammar School and from there to the Veterinary College in Edinburgh or Liverpool."

"You've got it all worked out."

"Yes, I mean to succeed," replied Mick.

"But everything's a muddle, because we may move again before Mick's taken all the exams. We want to live with Mum and Dad again. We want to find a house. But, you see, there has to be a job too," Katie said.

She saw a cottage, roses round the doorway; a picture postcard cottage with hollyhocks in the garden and a picturesque gate. It'll have three little bedrooms, she thought, and a sitting room where no-one has to sleep and a kitchen with a table in the middle, covered by a red-checked tablecloth. We'll be able to have a dog, and the twins will play in the garden and there'll be hens which lay lots and lots of warm brown eggs.

"They'll get used to living with me in time, you'll see," said Mrs Millet.

They had reached her house. Somewhere far away chickens cackled.

For an awful moment Mick thought that David Smith was going to drive away without saying goodbye.

He stood in the road, feeling small and dirty and young and hopelessly poor, and for a second he thought, I'll never get there. I'll never be a vet, never pass all those exams, never be anything ... He saw the years stretching ahead full of failure. It's over, he thought. Prince is going. For one day we tasted the pleasure of having a pony of our own. Now we must face life as it is ...

"Goodbye," he said, and was angry because tears of disappointment blinded his eyes.

Katie pressed her face against the trailer. "Goodbye, Prince, be good," she said. She thought, I don't care. I'm not going to care any more about anything; it's too exhausting and nothing ever works out right, not for us at any rate. Perhaps other people are luckier ... She thought of the girl they had seen with two ponies, the other one in the forge in her well-cut clothes. She saw now that her jeans were torn, and looking at Mick she noted his bloodstained knee. I wouldn't want to live through the last few hours again not for anything, she decided. And we're lucky no-one was angry over the broken window.

David looked at the children's dirty faces. "Don't be in such a hurry," he said. "I thought you were coming to the stables. The Canningtons may want to thank you officially; after all they don't know anything about you yet."

"But we didn't do anything, not really," Katie said.

"Why don't you come over on Saturday? I'm sure there are buses," David said.

The children looked at one another. Mick mouthed "Money. . ." and Katie nodded. They didn't know how to explain. Mrs Millet came to their rescue. "If it's money you're worrying about, your mother sent me some this morning. She said it was for extras. But are you safe to go on buses alone?"

"We came all the way here alone," Mick said.

"That's all right, then. Come as soon as you can on Saturday. Bring a picnic lunch. There won't be many other children, because we are mainly a dealing establishment. But at any rate you can have a look round. . . And thank you very much for looking after Blue Grass," They realised that David was really leaving this time. They stood waving, two dirty, bedraggled figures with smiles they didn't feel on their faces, feeling as though they were waving away hope.

"He's friendly, a nice lad altogether," announced

Mrs Millet. The children still stood like people in a dream.

"Come on. It's a hot meal and bed for both of you," cried Mrs Millet.

"What about school?" asked Katie.

"You'll have to miss that today. If I did send you, you wouldn't learn anything. You're both tired out, and no wonder. Really, kids . . ."

She pushed them towards the house.

"Well, we've got Saturday to look forward to at any rate," said Mick, half to himself.

Their places were still laid for breakfast in the kitchen, though the alarm clock which stood on the dresser told them that the time was a quarter to eleven.

"Now upstairs and into the bath, Katie, and quick. I'm going to give you each a tray in bed. Hurry now. There's Mick to follow."

Katie stumbled up the stairs, found the taps, ran the water. As Mick says, there's Saturday to look forward to and that is better than nothing, and Mrs Millet doesn't seem cross, thought Katie, peeling off her wet clothes, getting into the bath, seeing suddenly the old bath at home.

In the kitchen Mrs Millet said, "You'd better get your wet clothes off and put a towel round yourself, Mick. You'll both have colds tomorrow, that's certain. Oh, well never mind. Boys will be boys I suppose, though most of them won't look at a pony nowadays. It's motor bikes or cars all the way."

"Perhaps they want to be racing motorists, you know, like Stirling Moss," Mick replied.

He could understand that; he too was a lover of speed; and his father had been keen on motor bike races when he was a boy.

"If I didn't care for horses, it would be cars for me too," he said.

Chapter Twelve

SATURDAY MORNING

They were in school the next day. Mrs Millet had given them a letter to take, and no questions were asked. Their clothes were clean and dry by this time, and they were living only for Saturday.

They couldn't help telling the other children where they were going. "You must know Littleheath Stables," they insisted. "David Smith works there— you know, the man who's always on TV when there's a horse show. The one who started without any money . . ."

Just saying that gave them new hope, because, if David Smith had got so far without any money, why shouldn't they?

But most of the children had never heard of David Smith. "What is he, a footballer? A film star?" they asked.

The days passed slowly. They received a letter from their mother; in the evenings they watched TV before going to bed.

They were beginning to like Mrs Millet. "She could have been awful about us going out all night and all," Mick said.

"I know. She was really nice about it. Really she was . . ."

"Really she was," mimicked Mick.

They wrote to their mother.

"We haven't found a house yet, but we're keeping our ears open," wrote Mick.

"I think we ought to tell you about the lost pony," wrote Katie and filled three pages with a description of their ride, their night out, a portrait of the vet and of David.

Thursday passed, Friday came.

"Tomorrow we go," announced Mick.

"I'm so excited, but I don't suppose anything will happen," replied Katie.

"But it will be fun just to look at the horses," replied Mick.

Mrs Millet cleaned their shoes for the occasion.

"You'd better catch the nine o'clock bus. I'm afraid you'll have to change in Piddington. You'll want a No 47. The stop's opposite where you get off. Anybody will tell you," said Mrs Millet.

"I wish we had better clothes," sighed Katie.

"I hope he hasn't forgotten all about us," said Mick.

"I'll make you a big packet of sandwiches, and you can have an orange each," Mrs Millet told them.

The kitchen seemed more friendly by this time, and it was more untidy; the garden looked bright and clean after so much rain, and the weather had turned fine at last. Altogether the children felt that everything was on their side.

"Perhaps the Canningtons will be there," said Katie, imagining Mrs Cannington, beautiful in a fur coat, giving them a present.

"Don't expect too much. You'll only be disappointed," answered Mrs Millet.

She sent them early to bed, but they didn't sleep.

"I think it'll be fine tomorrow. There was a red sunset anyway," Mick whispered through the wall.

"It's a silly name for him. I much prefer Prince."

"Same here," answered Katie.

They slept at last, but were up at the first sign of dawn in the sky. They dressed carefully, hurried downstairs, put the kettle on.

"It's fine at any rate," Mick said.

They gobbled their breakfast, when at last it was ready.

"There's no need to rush so. You've still got an hour before the bus leaves," said Mrs Millet.

Even so, eight thirty found them running through the village to the bus stop.

"You'd better catch the bus; otherwise you'll have to walk through the town," Mrs Millet had said.

Now waiting impatiently, they wished they had chosen to walk.

The weather was certainly fine, and warm for October; they wore jeans, thick sweaters and trainers.

"Doesn't it seem years since we left home?" asked Mick.

"Yes. Wouldn't it be lovely if Mum and Dad were here . . ."

"One never gets everything," replied Mick philosophically.

"Other children do."

"I don't think so."

"I wish the bus would come."

At last other bus catchers appeared—a woman with empty shopping baskets, a man in a suit, a couple of girls. It heartened the children; they couldn't take their eyes off the road now.

"It must come soon," said Katie.

The girls talked quietly to one another. The man took a watch from his pocket and looked at it. The woman with the shopping baskets shifted her weight from one foot to the other.

"It's late," the man in the suit said.

"They don't bother about time any more. If you're early it's late and if you're on time it's already gone," complained the woman.

Two cars passed them, a man on a bicycle.

"I have to catch a train," the man said.

"That won't bother them," the woman answered.

"We'll miss our connection if it doesn't come soon," Mick told Katie.

The village seemed oddly quiet. They could see the postman delivering letters; a boy passed them on a pony.

"I hope nothing's happened," the woman said.

"I wish we had walked. We would have been there by now," announced Katie.

The man looked at his watch again.

"I shan't catch my train now," he muttered.

"I don't think it's coming," said one of the girls.

"Perhaps there's been a crash," replied the woman.

Katie was thinking, nothing goes right for us. Why doesn't the bus come? Please, God, make it come. She was feeling cold now, sick of waiting. We never have any luck, she thought.

It must come soon, thought Mick. It's going to come. I mustn't panic. Probably country buses don't run to time. We'll get to Littleheath Stables somehow.

"I shall walk in a minute," said the man, getting out his watch and looking at it.

"What's the time?" asked the woman.

"Nine fifteen."

"Something's wrong, then. I'll go home, again, I think. There's plenty to do about the house."

For a moment she stood wavering. Then she left them.

"It must come soon," Mick said.

"We'd better walk."

"It's too bad," said one of the girls.

Katie was trying not to cry; she felt somehow that the day was already doomed.

"Come on. We'd better run," said Mick.

They ran. "We've missed the other bus, anyway, haven't we? There's no point in hurrying," Katie said.

She was hating the whole expedition now—she had expected so much; instead, there was muddle and uncertainty. Our whole life is a muddle, if it comes to that, she thought. Other children live with their parents, have a real home which is really there ... "Wait, can't you?" she shouted angrily. "You know I can't run as fast as you can."

Mick was trying to control his feelings. He could feel rage and despair fighting for possession behind his calm outward countenance.

"The buses probably run every half-hour. We can

catch the next one," he yelled back over his shoulder. "If I get there first, I'll make it wait for you," he added on second thoughts.

If we catch one at half past ten, we won't be late. David only said to get to the stables as early as you can, he thought.

There were people still waiting at two of the stops that passed—three children in school uniform, a man in a boiler suit, a mother and toddler. They stood irresolutely, wondering whether to walk or to return home. The sun was shining by now, fulfilling the promise of the evening before.

Mick passed the station, and remembered his first glimpse of it; there were people waiting for a train, and the ticket-collector smiled at him. He was very hot in his jersey, so that sweat ran down his face, and he could feel his socks sticking to his feet.

He wasn't sure of the way now; but Mrs Millet said they'd have to walk straight through the town, so he kept right on. It wasn't much of a town in his opinion; it couldn't compare with his own town for shops and parks and breadth of streets. He saw a brewery horse which for a moment made him think of Nelly. He couldn't see any buses, but there were plenty of cars, and some of the shops were full to overflowing.

Behind him Katie was still running, but her feet seemed to be saying over and over again: It's no use. It's no use ... Often Mick quoted, "Seek and thou shalt find," but at this moment she didn't believe it; she only believed in luck and in her opinion the Smallbones didn't have any, and never had and probably never would.

Mick was a long way ahead and her legs were aching, and she couldn't see any buses, only people spending money—pounds and pounds, as though they grew on trees and one simply had to pick the notes. One of her ribbons had come out of her hair and she was much too hot in her thick jersey. And now she could see that people were staring at her, obviously thinking, whatever is she doing running like that straight through the town as though there was something after her? She didn't like being looked at, and she didn't like people to consider her peculiar; so she broke into a walk and thought, Mick will have to stew in his own juice. He should have waited for me. After all, he is the eldest.

Mick had reached a bus stop which said Country Buses and in small figures below, 47, 52, 21. He felt triumphant. He thought, We'll get there after all. We won't be late—for he could see a clock above the jewellers now which said ten to ten. He couldn't see Katie, but he wasn't worried because he was sure the No 47 bus must run on the hour and on the half-hour. There'll be other people coming to wait for it soon, he thought, and then: I should like to eat some of my lunch, but perhaps I'd better wait for Katie.

He thought, Why doesn't she run faster? I'm sure she could if she tried.

Katie could see Mick at last. She stopped to wave. He was waiting all alone at a stop. He looks peculiar, she thought. Why isn't there anyone else there? I can't see any buses anywhere, if it comes to that.

Mick was calling now: "Run. It goes in five min-

101

utes." Several people turned to look and someone shouted something out of a car window, but he had some sort of accent and Katie couldn't understand a word. She started to run again and knocked against a woman with a basket, who cried, "Look what you're doing dear. Where do you think you're going?"

"To catch a bus," answered Katie truthfully, which for some reason made the woman burst out laughing, and call after Katie, "If you're lucky."

She reached the bus stop.

"At last. I thought you were never coming."

"Well, I don't see a bus," replied Katie.

"It'll be along in a minute."

"How do you know?"

"It must be."

"I don't see anyone else waiting for it . . . And if it comes to that, I don't see any buses."

"Perhaps there aren't many."

"I wish we could sit down," Katie said. Her legs were aching, and suddenly she was certain that there wasn't going to be a bus.

"Today's been doomed from the start," she said.

"Don't be silly. It's not even dinner-time yet," replied Mick.

"Let's ask someone about the bus," Katie said. She turned to speak to a young woman pushing a baby in a pram. "Do you know when the No 47 bus comes please?" she asked.

The woman looked her up and down. "But didn't you know the bus men are out on strike?"

"You mean there aren't any?" cried Mick.

"That's right. They want a ten per cent rise."

They watched the woman pushing her pram away along the pavement.

"You see, that's just our luck," said Katie unable to keep bitterness from her voice. "We might as well give up."

"You can if you like. I'm not going to."

They turned to face one another.

"I wish we had never come to the country. Really I do," cried Katie.

"I'm not giving in. I'm going to get to the Littleheath Stables today even if I have to walk there," said Mick.

"But it's miles."

"I don't care. . ."

"Well, let's have something to eat before we start," said Katie in a resigned voice.

"The best things in life are always difficult to get," said Mick.

"How do you know?"

"Dad told me that once."

"Not for some people."

"You and some people," sighed Mick. They ate their sandwiches, ignoring the busy shoppers who turned to look at them.

"Now, where next?" asked Mick.

"We don't even know where the stables are," complained Katie.

"Well, we can find out, can't we? Once we know where the No 47 buses go when they're running, we're half-way there," Mick said.

"What about the walking?" Katie asked.

"Running, you mean. Perhaps we'll get a lift," Mick said.

Chapter Thirteen

THE STABLES

They started to run, stopping at intervals to ask, "Is this where the No 47 bus goes from?"

They lost all sense of time.

Then suddenly Katie cried, "Supposing we're going in the wrong direction?"

"How can we be?" replied Mick.

"If the bus runs straight through the town to somewhere bigger."

They nearly lost their nerve then. It was the thought of Blue Grass which kept them going. The short time during which they had looked after him had only increased their desire to ride, until now it was almost the only thing which mattered.

They ran, praying that they were going in the right direction, and the pale October sun shone on them, and every time they turned a corner they hoped to see a sign which read the Littleheath Stables.

Katie started to lose heart first.

"I don't think we're ever going to get there. It must be nearly lunch-time," she said. Her legs didn't seem to belong to her any more by this time, and her head was throbbing.

"Well, let's finish our sandwiches first."

"I'm so thirsty," she complained.

"We'll knock at a door, ask for water and ask whether they know the stables," Mick said.

They took off their jerseys, slung them round their necks and ate their sandwiches.

Cars passed them; they all had a holiday air, and nearly all the back seats were full of children.

"We haven't tried for a lift yet," Mick said.

"Remember what Mum said."

"We can choose a car with several people inside; after all, we don't take up much room."

They were still hungry when they had finished their sandwiches; it was the sort of hunger which sandwiches doesn't dispel—it called for hot, filling food, for roast beef and Yorkshire pudding, a plate of bacon and eggs or an enormous tea.

"Now for a house," Mick said.

They were on a big road. Signs read to Birmingham and the North. For a long time there were fields on each side. They nearly asked a lorry-driver eating his lunch in a lay-by, but they remembered their mother's oft-repeated warnings, and after a short, whispered consultation, they continued along the road.

"I don't even know which county we're in," Katie said. "How shall we find our way home?"

"Nothing difficult in that," Mick said.

They came to some bungalows at last, and ran down the path of the first one with renewed strength in their legs. Net curtains hid the interior. They knocked on the door and a dog barked. There were gnomes in the garden, a sundial on the lawn. A woman opened the door.

"What do you want?" she asked. "I haven't any windfall apples, so it's no good you asking, and I never give anything for the guy. Don't say you're starting to sing carols already."

"We only wanted a drink of water," Mick said.

"Are you sure? She eyed them suspiciously. "There's so many burglaries, it's not safe to let anybody in nowadays. You'd better stay by the door and I'll fetch you some water." She moved away reluctantly.

"She doesn't like us," Mick said.

"I'm not surprised. You look terrible. Really you do," answered Katie. She was near to tears. She wasn't sure that she even wanted to reach the stables now.

They drank a glass of water each, and asked the way to the stables.

"Keep straight on. You'll see the sign. But it's a long way yet," she said, shutting the door in their faces.

They felt like shouting with triumph then: because they were on the right road; because sooner or later, if they kept running, they'd reach the stables.

"We'd better walk for a bit, or we'll get a stitch," said Mick, shutting the garden gate after them.

"Perhaps we won't be so late after all. I wish we had asked the time," cried Katie.

Presently they were running again, on and on along the same enormous, endless road.

We'll dream of this; it'll be one of our nightmares,

this straight, modern road, and our running feet, and the sign we never see, decided Katie.

We must get there soon, thought Mick. His feet were aching, and his left heel was blistered. For the first time he considered whether they were mad to be so determined to reach the Littleheath Stables. Supposing David simply showed them round and wished them goodbye? How would they feel, walking home? How would they bear the disappointment? And how blank their future would seem!

But whatever happens I'm still going to get to the Grammar School, Mick decided. Nothing must shake my determination to be a vet. I shall specialise in horses, he thought, and when I earn enough to keep a horse I shall buy one.

"Look," cried Katie in a terrified voice. "There's a police car signalling to us to stop."

They both thought of the window. Katie saw them in Court, a woman police officer on each side of them, judges in wigs. They'll say we're in need of care and attention, decided Mick. They'll send us away and we'll never see Prince or David again.

"Wait a minute, will you?" called a policeman, leaning out of the car window.

They waited while the car drew into the kerb, and for a moment time seemed to stand still, and Katie saw her mother reading a letter from a probation officer, and Mick imagined David waiting for them in vain.

The policeman stepped out of the car; one of them, (whom Katie automatically thought of as the head one), flicked out a notebook. "Your names, please?"

he said. "Brother and sister, eh?" he asked, writing them down.

"You don't come from these parts, do you?" asked the other. "I can tell that by your voices."

"We're only staying here with foster-parents until Mum and Dad can find a house."

"Well, what are you doing on this road? We've been observing you for some time. You're not by any chance running away, are you?" It was the head one who spoke.

Mick was suddenly furious. As if we would do that, he thought.

"We're on our way to the Littleheath Stables!" he cried indignantly. "There are no buses, so we're walking." He was surprised by his own sudden anger. But it's the last straw, he thought. As if it isn't bad enough about the buses without this too.... "We're late already," he said.

"We'll take you there at any rate," said the head one, suddenly smiling. "I've got two kids myself and they're mad about this horse business. We're on the lookout for a boy and a girl. That's why we stopped you. But your appearance doesn't tally. You're too small by half, and too alike. They're not brother and sister. Now hop in."

The children felt very sumptuous in the back of the police car. Katie couldn't help wondering what her school friend, Sophie, would say if she knew.

Mick was more interested in the time.

"It's after lunch, isn't it?" he asked.

"It's twenty to three," replied the head one.

"Oh dear, we are late!" cried Katie.

They seemed to be travelling very fast—faster than they had ever been before in a car, decided Katie.

"Do you like it here?" asked the policeman.

"It's all right," answered Mick, and he couldn't keep disappointment from his voice, because he had expected so much — a dog in the Millet's house, a chance to ride, perhaps even a pony of his own; instead, the country had yielded Prince, one disaster after another and now finally the bus strike. Suddenly he was tired of it all, of being wet and tired, of never having what he wanted.

"It's not much different from the town; only cleaner," he added, ignoring the beauty of the rolling fields on each side of them, the grey stone farmsteads, the softness of the blue October sky.

"We miss Mum and Dad," Katie said.

"I expect you do," replied the head policeman.

They could see the sign now which had eluded them for so long. It stood out bright and clean and white; black letters announced The Littlehealth Stables, and beyond the sign they saw rough land with heather and gorse, and trees which were squat and shrivelled like people old before their time.

"We'll drop you here. You can manage the drive, can't you?"

"Yes easily." They jumped out of the car. At long last they had arrived, and at that moment the miles they had walked were forgotten; only the drive was there, winding and gravelled, and beyond that the stables, David and Prince.

"Thanks a lot," they cried.

"Fancy getting a lift from a police car," said Katie. They started to run again.

"It must be nearly three," Mick said.

Katie was already visualising their arrival. David Smith crying, "At last! I thought you were never coming." The Canningtons might even be there; and that would mean they had met real film stars—she'd have to write and tell Sophie about that. And then there was Prince, or, to be more correct, Blue Grass. He would recognise them and neigh, and there would be all the other horses to look at, perhaps even a ride. A hundred possibilities rushed to her mind, and then they could see the stables, rows of modern loose-boxes; there was a paddock running alongside the drive, just as Katie had visualised—full of jumps, black, formidable brush fences, gates, triple bars, doubles, red and grey walls, even a bank and a water-jump.

They stopped to stare at these.

"They're just like the ones on TV," Katie said.

"It's where they train their jumpers," Mick answered before they started to run again; and now they could see each horse individually, or rather, their heads and necks.

"Aren't there a lot?" cried Katie.

"Mrs Millet said it was a big stable."

"I shall work at a place like this one day."

They stood and looked round the yard. There was no-one in sight and they saw now that many of the loose-box doors were open.

"I feel I belong to a place like this," Katie said.

"Same here," agreed Mick.

"I don't see David."

"Let's see if we can find Prince."

They felt a little flat now, because there was no-one to greet them. As usual, we've expected too much, thought Katie.

They started to walk round the horses, stopping to pat each shining neck.

"However do they get them so glossy and shining?" asked Katie.

"Elbow grease and the right food," replied Mick.

They found Prince at last in a little loose-box behind the others next to a brown pony. He didn't whinny when they called his name, nor did he seem pleased to see them; and that was just one more disappointment in a disappointing day. For some reason, they started to feel like trespassers then; if he had welcomed them everything would have been all right; now they felt as though they had arrived expecting a party on the wrong day. Katie was over-whelmed by gloom from that moment. It's just as I thought—nothing ever goes right for us, she thought.

"We'd better go home," she said.

"What do you mean? We've got to find David first."

"He isn't here." There was a choke in Katie's voice now, and a large tear rolled down her grimy cheek.

She felt as though it was the end of the world; the end of everything.

"He must be somewhere."

"He's forgotten all about us," Katie answered.

"Don't be such a dummy," cried Mick, determined not to believe his sister's words. "If he isn't here now, he will be soon. Remember we're late."

"What are we to do then?"

"Wait."

"In another hour it'll be dark. We must think of Mrs Millet."

"We can find a phone-box. We've still our bus money."

They started to walk round the horses again, imagining they owned them all, and now dusk was coming, and they realised that soon they must leave without having seen David. They stopped talking then and each retreated into a private world. Mick started to make plans for another visit; Katie thought of home and how they would have been better occupied looking for a house to let. The yard seemed to grow quieter. Some of the horses were dozing standing up, their lower lips hanging loosely, like pouches waiting to be filled.

"We'd better go," said Mick at last. And silently and hopelessly Katie began to cry, and they were both suddenly afraid of the long walk home.

"I wish we had never come. Really I do," said Katie.

"We'll come again next Saturday. Perhaps the buses will be running again by then. We've still got our money; that's the main thing," Mick said. He didn't mean to be defeated. We'll keep coming until we see David again, he thought.

They turned to go and knew suddenly how tired they were. Mrs Millet must know about the bus strike by now, decided Katie. Perhaps she'll ask the police to look for us. I wonder whether anyone has reported the broken window. How far away from home I feel. I suppose Sophie is walking back from the park. Mum must be getting tea, unless she's feeding the twins.

They walked very slowly along the drive. And the jumps didn't interest them now, and Mick's heels grew more painful each moment, until at last he said, "I think I'll walk barefoot."

"You can't; everyone will stare," replied Katie.

But he took off his shoes and socks just the same. Katie thought with shame, what would Mum say if she could see us? We look like child tramps.

"It's much better. Why don't you take off yours too?" Mick asked.

But Katie wouldn't, and so they walked on through the approaching evening, not noticing anything, beyond their tired feet and aching legs.

And Katie thought, it's all over now; this long, dreary walk is reality. While Mick said to himself, it doesn't matter. All this will pass; good days will come and then we'll be united again—Katie and myself with Mum and Dad and the twins.

They were so tired that sometimes they felt as though they walked in dream; that soon they'd wake and be at home with the roar of traffic outside the window, and the street lamps glowing warm in the dusk.

It was a long time before they reached the point where the police car had picked them up, and they both knew how long and endless was the road after that. They sat down for a moment on the grass verge which ran alongside the road, and Katie said, "What about that phone call?"

"We'd better look out for a phone box," replied Mick.

They started to walk again and now the passing cars had their lights on, and somehow the road seemed smaller in the darkening dusk. "I don't believe in anything any more; not in myself," Katie said suddenly. "Probably I shall take a job in a factory when I leave school."

"Don't be so daft. We'll be living in the country by then," cried Mick who wanted to believe that. He could still see them all together in one of the many bungalows they has passed; the twins riding tricycles round the garden, himself helping Dad with the digging; Katie making little cakes with Mum in the bright modern kitchen there would be at the back, looking out on the vegetable garden full of beans and peas and young trees; perhaps even a strawberry bed.

And then suddenly they heard the sound of hoofs behind them, and they couldn't believe their ears, until at last they turned and saw a horse galloping along the verge towards them in the dusk.

Katie said, "We'd better get out of the way." But Mick staring steadily into the dusk, cried: "It's David Smith!"

Chapter Fourteen

IT'S TRUE

He stopped beside them, and suddenly everything was real and wonderful again.

"I'm sorry I missed you. I suppose the bus strike made you late. I wanted to show you round the horses," David said. His mount was a fidgety bay, which played with her bit, and swished her tail, and kept pawing the ground as though longing to be galloping again.

"How did you know we'd been?"

"That was a piece of luck if you like. I saw a police car, which I stopped because I wanted to tell them about the Cannington's window, and the Inspector told me about you, said he had dropped a boy and a girl at the stables, and, of course, I knew at once that it could only be you," replied David.

"It's a change for us to have any luck. Really it is," said Katie.

"Well, there's some more coming," said David. "I've found somewhere for you to live."

The children couldn't speak for a minute. Then Mick asked, "You mean for all of us?"

"Of course, that is if your parents like the country."

"Dad does; he lived in the country when he was a

boy," replied Mick with pride in his voice, as though to live in the country was something special, something to give you a feeling of pride.

"But there has to be work," said Katie, who, now the first moment of surprise was disappearing, could see nothing but difficulties. "And he doesn't care a great deal for horses; that is, he wouldn't want to be a groom."

"I'm not suggesting that; let's all sit down on the verge and get down to brass tacks; then you or I can write a letter to your parents."

They knew now that he was in earnest; that something wonderful was happening.

They sat down together on the verge, and David let the bay mare crop the grass and said, "There's a man who owns a market garden a few miles from the stables; he's run it himself for a good many years, but now he's having trouble with his heart and the doctors say he mustn't do hard work any more."

"You mean Dad ought to become a gardener?" cried Katie.

"Not exactly that; better really," said David, stopping to push a lock of hair off his forehead. "Mr Stone wants someone to run his place; and they can have his house too, because he's not to walk up stairs any more, so he's building himself a bungalow. It'll be hard work, of course, but there's a van to take the vegetables to the station, and a pony to generally help about the place."

"A pony!" cried the children.

"I thought that would interest you," said David. "Of course, your father may not like the suggestion,

or there's a chance Mr Stone may not like your
father, but I don't think that's likely, because I
expect your father's something like you: you must
have got your resourcefulness and common sense
from somewhere."

The children weren't used to compliments, Katie
wasn't even certain what 'resourcefulness' meant.

"What do you think?" asked David.

"Well, it really depends on Dad. It sounds smash-
ing to me," said Mick.

Katie was determined to keep her imagination
within strict bounds; she had hoped for too much too
often. This time she didn't mean to be disappointed.

Mick felt differently. "But he must accept it," he
cried. "Think a pony!"

"Don't think the pony will be like Blue Grass; he's
just an old cart pony with creaking joints. Once he
pulled the roller on the local cricket pitch. But he'll
do to learn on. I started on something very much the
same," said David, remembering himself as a small
boy; how shy he had been; how little he had known
about life; he had mostly lived in a dream full of
horses and success, and somehow it had all come
true.

"Never give up; that's my advice to you. If you
want something badly enough you'll get it in the end.
But I expect you know that; otherwise you wouldn't
have stuck to Blue Grass as you did," said David,
standing up, suddenly feeling old again beside these
two children, one with bare feet, and both with
small, exhausted faces.

"We must get going. Here, you have the first ride,

Katie, since you're the only girl present," David said, tightening the bay mare's girth.

"Are you coming with us, then?" asked Mick.

"Well, I'm not going to let you walk all the way by yourselves. You'd better put your shoes on, Mick."

He gave Katie a leg up, and she felt very high sitting on the beautiful forward-cut saddle, holding the reins, looking at the bay mare's neat ears.

"But what about you getting home? Is it all right to ride along this road in the dark?" asked Mick, who felt quite wildly happy, and whose imagination was already racing ahead, seeing them riding to hounds, learning to jump, grooming a pony which they could almost call their own.

"She's mine. She's Tornado. I often ride her in the dark. I have to exercise her when I can. I shall ride her home across country, and if there's a moon I shall put her over a few fences on the way."

They were walking now. Katie was saying to herself over and over again: it's true. It really is happening. I'm riding the famous Tornado. Everything is going to be all right after all. Her feelings of exhaustion had gone, leaving in its place a sense of exultation.

Mick was right, she thought, the Lost Pony was the beginning of everything; it was a kind of miracle.

Katie and Mick took it in turns to ride; and now it was quite dark, and the only sound was that of cars, and the steady clip-clop of Tornado's hoofs. And the children were at peace; it no longer mattered that they had left home; that Mr Millet might hit them, as he had threatened once; if nothing ever came of

David's suggestion, this ride home on Tornado would be with them for always.

"What if Mr Stone doesn't like us riding his pony?" asked Mick once.

"He says he doesn't mind. I've asked him already. There really isn't any work for the pony to do now that there's the van," David answered.

But for the most part they walked in companionable silence, and gradually the sounds of night in the country filled their ears; the croak of a frog, the call of a fox, the screech of an owl, and most of all, the sound of cows' rough tongues eating the last of the autumn grass.

They came at last to Piddington, and here the street lamps and the lighted shop windows gave a festive air to the little town. It was after that they started to sing, quietly, all at once, beginning with 'Three Wheels on my Wagon.' And then quite suddenly they had reached the house. They had agreed by this time that both David and the children would write to Mr Smallbone.

"Will you be all right now?" David asked.

"Yes, thank you."

The children didn't know how to put what they felt into words.

"And thank you for everything," said Katie as David mounted.

"That's all right. I'll ride over and let you know what your father says to my letter."

They watched him ride away before they turned to the house and the row they were certain awaited them.

Mrs Millet was ironing.

"So you've consented to come home at last," she said. Her voice was hard and very cold. "Well, Katie and Mick Smallbone, I've given you enough chances. This is the end. You'll go just as soon as I can arrange it." She devoured them with her eyes, staring at their tired faces with disgust.

"You'd better sit down and I'll get you some supper. Goodness knows I've done my best. Why can't you behave like other children? I suppose that's why your mother sent you away . . ." She moved towards the oven. "I've done my best," she repeated.

"We're going, anyway," said Mick, and couldn't keep the happiness and triumph from his voice. "David had found us a house and Dad a job and there's a pony too."

"And that's a likely tale, I'm sure," replied Mrs Millet.

"But it's true," cried Mick.

"Tell me another."

They could not stand up to her. Her sarcasm was worse than a slap in the face.

"Anyway the Health Visitor's most likely coming tonight; perhaps the local Social Worker too."

They froze then. "I'm sorry," whispered Katie; and she thought, happiness never lasts; perhaps it's not meant to. She's spoiling everything.

"It's a bit late to say that. It's not that I don't like you; don't think that. You've got pluck and plenty; but I'm here to look after you . . ."

There was a knock on the front door.

"That'll be the Health Visitor," said Mrs Millet.

She went to the door in her slippers and the children sat close together, trying not to cry. They had half expected this, but they weren't prepared to meet it—not now, exhausted from their long walk.

"Come in, Miss Brown."

"There are two ladies," whispered Katie.

"I know," murmured Mick, who was trying to assemble points for his defence. He didn't know what they could say. At this moment there seemed no real excuse for their behaviour of the last few days.

"I didn't like asking you to come," Mrs Millet was saying. "But really I was at my wits' end. I nearly called the police. It's not that I don't like the kids. Please don't think that."

She started to tell the two visitors what had occurred since the children's arrival; and it sounded an extraordinary story, though true enough. It was a story full of 'I said' and 'they said', punctuated by "It's not that I don't like the kids, Don't think that."

Katie liked the look of the Social Worker, who was fat and motherly, with neat grey hair. Mick was trying desperately to think of a reply; the trouble was there was nothing to answer, because everything Mrs Millet said was true.

Katie was glad that Mr Millet was missing. She thought, to use a term her mother used, that he would have added fuel to the fire.

"It's just this urge they've got; they must be with a pony. What I was wondering was whether you could find them some different foster-parents, perhaps someone with stables or a farm," finished Mrs Millet. The children realised then, quite suddenly, that she was their friend, that even if she had called these two people in a moment of rage, she was now on their side.

"But what about this house and the job David Smith has found? Surely that is the best thing that could have happened in the circumstances," said the grey-haired Social Worker.

Katie and Mick began to tell their side of the story then, and when they had finished the Health Visitor said: "I have a reliable friend in London. Why don't I get her to call on Mr Smallbone and find out his reaction to the suggested job? Then we'd know where we stand, and if this job falls through maybe we can find another . . ."

"That sounds a very good suggestion," replied the Social Worker. "But will you behave in the meantime, Katie and Mick? You see we're doing the best we can for you."

"But yes, of course. There's no pony to look after now anyway. . ." said Mick.

"The earliest we can let you know is Monday morning, Mrs Millet," the Health Visitor said. "Either way I'll be round to see you."

"Thank you very much. I'm sorry I bothered you, but it makes you anxious, them not being my kids and all," replied Mrs Millet.

And now the visitors were leaving. "We'd better thank them," Mick muttered to Katie; and the children made a little speech full of 'sorrys' and 'thank yous'.

"There, and don't say I haven't done my best for you in the long run, though you don't deserve it. Now get out of those thick jerseys and have something to eat," said Mrs Millet, slamming the front door; shutting out the black night which had been with the children for so many hours. But now suddenly, they were too tired for anything; they only wanted the comfort of bed and sleep.

The children overslept the next morning, but even so the day seemed endless. They went backwards and forwards over the last few days, and when they had finished doing that, they started to think about the future, to make plans, to try and see themselves in a modern house, helping their father with the garden. "I shall pick the flowers," Katie said.

"I shall help with the soft fruits—you know, the strawberries and raspberries," Mick answered.

"And in the evening we shall ride," Katie said, and to say it gave her a warm feeling of security and happiness.

"And it'll never rain," said Mick.

"Now you're being silly."

"Well, I said the Lost Pony was the beginning of something, and I was right," Mick replied.

"If only today was over," sighed Katie.

But Monday came at last, and with it school.

"The whole day to get through before we know," grumbled Katie as they left the house in the morning.

"He can't say no."

"Mum may not like the idea."

And from that moment they were certain that their father would refuse the house and job. The thought haunted them so much that Mick upset his paints and Katie failed to do the simplest sum. It was like a sickness which kills all power of concentration; suddenly the day became like a nightmare of suspense.

And then, during break, the Head called them outside.

"Your foster-mother's here to see you," she said.

Katie felt sick, her legs shook under her, and there was a choking sensation in her throat.

Mick cried, "Thank you," and ran out of the classroom.

They found Mrs Millet wearing her apron.

"Well, it's thumbs up so far. I thought you'd like to know. Your father's very keen on the job, and your mother, too. It seems they've been missing you a lot. Your father hopes to be over tomorrow."

"You think he's going to take the job?" cried Mick.

"Everything points that way."

"Oh, isn't it wonderful," cried Katie.

"It's as good as winning on the pools," said Mick.

"Well I thought you'd like to know. I'll be off now. I was here when I was a kid, and to tell the truth this place always gives me the creeps."

The children thanked Mrs Millet; and they stood making plans in whispers, and Katie thought, tomorrow we'll see Dad. And Mick thought, as I said, The Lost Pony was the beginning. Now lots of things can happen, but whatever does I'm still going to be a vet. We've got so many friends now, thought Katie: David, Mrs Millet, Father Ambrose, the Health Visitor, the nice Social Worker. Perhaps we were right to look after Prince as we did, though we should have told the police. They all seem to be on our side. We've never had so many friends before.

The school bell was ringing now; break was over.

"From today we must turn over a new leaf; or else we'll be getting a bad name," Mick told Katie.

"It seems years since we left home, but it's only just over a week. Really it is," said Katie.

They were sent to their classrooms; and now they looked quite different; so that Mick's class turned to stare at him, and Katie's teacher said, "You look like the cat which swallowed the cream" and then, "But wake up" for Katie didn't seem to hear; for at that moment she was seeing a pony with creaking joints under an apple tree; round his hoofs crawled the twins, Katie's arms were filled with flowers and Mick held a basket brimming with strawberries. And it's all going to happen, she thought. It isn't a dream— it's true.

FOR WANT OF A SADDLE

For Want of A Saddle is the exciting sequel to *The Lost Pony*. You can follow the further adventures of Mick and Katie when they are re-united with their parents and the twins at their new home in the country. They have a pony to ride but can't afford a saddle. How are they to find one? Suddenly after a series of dramas and disappointments their dreams finally come true.

For Want Of A Saddle is available now at £3.25